MW00878264

A REDEEMING C(

The Beautiful World

Adapted from Eleanor H. Porter's Inspirational Novel: Just David

SUSAN ROHRER

THE BEAUTIFUL WORLD:
Adapted from Eleanor H. Porter's
Inspirational Novel: *Just David*
(A Redeeming Contemporary Classic)

Written by Susan Rohrer,
based on her screenplay adaptation of *Just David*

Kindly direct inquiries about novel or screenplay to:
InfiniteArtsMgmt@gmail.com

Readers may contact author at:
pinterest.com/IAMsusanrohrer

Brief Scripture in this book is quoted from the American Standard Version of the Bible and is drawn from the public domain.

Cover Images: Courtesy of morgueFile

Author Photo: Jean-Louis Darville

ISBN 13: 978-1508447399
ISBN 10: 150844739X

Rohrer's novel, The Beautiful World: An Adaptation of Eleanor H. Porter's Inspiration Novel: Just David:

Infinite Arts Media

1 2 3 4 5 6 7 8 9 10

Published in the United States of America

First Edition 2015

To all who find joy
in making this world so beautiful

Contents

About This Book	9
Chapter 1	15
Chapter 2	31
Chapter 3	49
Chapter 4	65
Chapter 5	77
Chapter 6	95
Chapter 7	111
Chapter 8	133
Chapter 9	147
Chapter 10	161

Chapter 11	173
Chapter 12	189
Chapter 13	201
Chapter 14	215
Chapter 15	231
Chapter 16	251
Chapter 17	269
Chapter 18	281
Chapter 19	291
Chapter 20	303
About the Authors	321

About This Book

It is with great admiration that I echo the esteemed author Eleanor H. Porter's luminous literary classic, *Just David,* through this contemporary retelling: *The Beautiful World.* My sincere hope is to introduce Porter's stirring story to new generations, through both the motion picture screenplay and the novel adaptations she inspired me to write.

While a unique and comprehensive rewrite of *Just David*, *The Beautiful World* faithfully builds on the firm foundation of Porter's work, encouraging it beyond its auspicious beginnings in 1916 when it found even greater popularity than her earlier novel, *Pollyanna*, which inspired multiple feature films and television remakes.

In adapting *Just David* for twenty-first century readers, *The Beautiful World* further explores mysteries Porter's original novel only ventured to suggest. Rather than focusing solely on ten-year-old David's point of view, *The Beautiful World* delves into the complicated relationships of her adult characters, kindling loves old and new, mingling the beloved heart of this time-honored classic with contemporary life. While remaining faithful to the emotional core of *Just David*, some events and characterizations have been respectfully retooled in order to suit the contemporary milieu.

From my first reading years ago, it was clear to me that there is much more to Porter's underlying classic novel than meets the casual eye. Why else has *Just David* been made required reading by so many teachers? Why would her book have inspired countless parents to name their sons *David* after its soulful protagonist, to scour old bookstores for copies to pass on to friends and family? Why would this story have motivated untold would-be violinists to set impassioned bows to strings all over the globe?

It is not so much that we see ourselves in David, as much as we might hope that we could. Rather, it is that we find ourselves in the stubborn pride of workaholic farmer Simeon Holly, and in the utter loneliness of his dutiful wife, Ellen. We recognize single mother Tina Glaspell as she toils to make ends meet. We resonate with the truncated career path of Jack Gurnsey, and the aching for purpose of his estranged childhood sweetheart, heiress Barbara Holbrook.

Like each of these pivotal characters, something in us responds to the hope that dawns in the form of young David, and the prospect of experiencing life as abundantly as he does. That is the power of this remarkable story. It has the potential—quietly and covertly—to transform.

Though wildly successful in its day, Porter's inspirational book has drifted from the limelight of present culture. Those who have unearthed this treasure adore it. They pass it down through the generations, allowing themselves to go back to a time before childlike innocence fell prey to the jaded corruption of the post-modern world.

The contrast between innocence and guile may be even starker today than it was when Porter first penned the original. In the present day, we find the pure-hearted David to be even more of an arresting oddity. We haven't a clue what to make of his wondrous ways.

In the face of eroding ethics, economic peril, rampant unemployment, and a universal longing for meaning in life, David's boundless appreciation for nature and music, and his effervescent journey to find beauty and purpose are all the more relevant than ever.

These values pose a challenge to every man, woman, and child. They resonate with the jubilance of David's violin, to all who dare to believe that goodness, innocence, and beauty are still possible in this beautiful world.

"...and a little child shall lead them."

Isaiah 11:6

A mountain stream glistened in the afternoon sun, tumbling down smoothed stones. Merrily, the strains of a violin erupted, as if describing the abounding wonders: the cascade of a misty waterfall over mossy banks, a pheasant refreshing herself in the cool water, then spreading her wings to take flight.

Ten-year-old David bounded up the rocks toward the summit. Reaching the crest, David raised a hand to shield his eyes, then scanned his vast surroundings.

Far to the north, a host of skyscrapers stood sentinel over a great city. Closer to the east, a lengthy train snaked across the rural valley below, where farmhouses scattered around a small town. That familiar silver river wound its way through fertile fields.

David let out a jubilant shout. "Hello, river!" His heart filled. If he didn't play all that creation inspired, he would simply burst. A melody rose from his violin, expressing everything that words could not. Nimble hands poured out their passion as David's bow crossed the taut strings of a well-worn instrument.

Joyfully, David described the sparkling river on his violin. Transitioning, he told of those towering pines, swaying in the breeze against cottony clouds, adrift across azure skies. He filled his lungs with fresh, mountain air. "Hello, cloud-boats! Look at you sailing up there."

David turned his gaze toward a modest log cabin, situated alone in a clearing. The dwelling he shared with his father perched far above the hubbub of the distant world below. David's heart swelled in his chest.

Home.

It always had been, to his recollection.

In a flash, David scampered down a footpath leading to the cabin. Daddy would expect him soon.

He set his violin down outside and grabbed some split wood from their pile. Surely, the fire needed to be stoked by now.

Daddy usually kept a blaze going. But he hadn't been feeling so well the last week or so. David would fix him a nice supper. Daddy always appreciated that.

BEANS SIMMERED IN A CAST IRON SKILLET. Invitingly, their aroma filled the one room cabin. Books and sheet music splayed about, scattered among a collection of pinecones—treasures discovered over the course of many an exploration. Stacks of photographs flanked the aged family Bible they read from most mornings, except when Daddy needed to sleep longer, like today.

David called out to his slumbering father. "Daddy..."

His father didn't stir. Concerned, David left the stove. "Daddy, wake up!" David gave Daddy's shoulder a gentle nudge. "I've done the beans all by myself and the potatoes and your coffee, too. Quick, it'll get cold."

Finally, his father turned bleary eyes on him. "David... Aren't you David?"

"Well, of course, I'm David. Who else would I be? Come on." David gave Daddy's hands a tug.

Unsteadily, Daddy rose. "All right, now." He shuffled across the packed dirt floor to the table, fashioned from a felled oak.

David served up a steaming plate and set it down in front of his father. "The beans, they're not so good as yours, Daddy. Like you say, I might be a little out of tune with the Orchestra today."

"They're fine," Daddy said. "Just fine."

"Somehow, part of the stove got hotter than the rest and the water steamed out of the potatoes. But I'll do better next time. I promise."

Reluctantly, Daddy shook his head. "I'm afraid there won't be a next time."

David set the skillet aside. "Aren't you going to let me try again?"

"Well, Son..." Daddy drew in a labored breath. "This isn't a very nice way to start your supper, is it? Now, let's you and I say a word of thanks, so we can try some of your potatoes."

DAVID AND DADDY SAT OUTSIDE on a hand-hewn bench, watching the sinking sun shimmer over a distant lake in the valley.

"Look, Daddy, it's gold tonight. My silver lake is all gold with the sun."

Daddy winced.

That happened more and more these days. Not much helped. Except music. The balm of David's strings soothed Daddy like nothing else. David leapt to his feet and ran for his violin. "I'll play it for you, Daddy. The sunset." Not a moment passed before David set his instrument at his chin, painting the majesty of the evening skies.

Daddy drank it in, like the best kind of medicine. Still, a tortured look overtook him. "We have to give it up, you and I."

David turned wonderingly. "Give what up?"

"This," Daddy said. "All of this."

He lowered his bow. "What do you mean? This is home."

"It has been." Daddy massaged his knuckles. "But David...you didn't think we could always live here on the mountain like this, did you?"

"What better place could there be?" It seemed beyond imagining. What could be more idyllic than staying right where they were? "I like it, Daddy."

Weakly, his father inhaled.

David tried to think. "Should I gather some moss for that special tea tonight? You know that helps sometimes."

Daddy nodded thoughtfully. "Do you realize how long we've been here, Son?"

David mulled it over. "Always."

"Six years," Daddy corrected. "I brought you here when you were barely four, but I suppose you don't remember much."

He searched his mind. "Not really."

"For six years you've been all mine," Daddy said. "Mine to feed. Mine to clothe, to teach and protect. And in that time, what I've tried to do, what

I've meant for you is that only what is good and beautiful should have a place in your life."

David twirled a pine needle between his fingertips.

"It's not that I intended that evil or ugliness, even death shouldn't be defined for you," Daddy said. "It just seemed to me, that...if what's good and beautiful, well, if those things filled your thoughts... Then, maybe there wouldn't be room for anything else." Daddy stretched his spine. "That was my plan, for what it's worth. And I do think I've succeeded so completely that now—especially with how sick I'm getting—I'm beginning to doubt the wisdom of it."

Daddy turned to him, even more intently than before. "David, listen to me." He cast his eyes across the expanse before them. "Out there, there's a great big world to experience. There are men and women and other children waiting for you."

"For me?"

"It's been hitting me for a while," Daddy said. "I've never been more certain of anything than I am of this, David. So, hear me. You have a beautiful work to do in your life. And you can't do what you're meant to do all alone on a mountaintop."

David fixed a dreamy gaze on the colorful sky. "I think I'd like it. To go out there, into the world. If I could sail away on that cloud-boat."

A rattle escaped Daddy's chest. "I'm afraid we can't go on cloud-boats, Son. We'll have to hike a long way. I need to get you back, back to the world before..." Slowly, Daddy lumbered to his feet. He steadied himself against the bench, then pressed his fingertips to his temples.

Was this another dizzy spell? "Daddy?"

"Tomorrow, David. You and I... We've got to go tomorrow."

A dark sedan circled the stately drive arcing in front of Sunnycrest Estate.

Barbara Holbrook brushed her auburn locks aside to peer out a tinted window. At twenty-nine, to call the sprawling manor and its manicured gardens home seemed an overstatement. It hadn't even been her aunt's home. Not really.

Aunt Grace Holbrook had been far too humble to countenance such a regal lifestyle of her own choice. The woman hadn't had a pretentious bone in that sturdy frame of hers. But the estate had been willed to Aunt Grace long ago, after the passing of

Barbara's parents, as a place to rear their orphaned child.

Aunt Grace had been the one vestige of comfort after that terrible day. And now, even she had gone, leaving Barbara little choice but to return to the outskirts of the sleepy town of Hinsdale. And to rumble through the echoing halls of Sunnycrest alone.

Tina Glaspell emerged from the front door, an apron cinched around her waist. No doubt, she would hope to be kept on staff as housekeeper. Who could blame the woman? As a single mother raising two young children in this flagging economy, little reliable work came available to Tina, except tending to other people's houses. How else could Tina feed her daughter, Betsy, and Betsy's blind little brother, Joe? But how long could Barbara endure this place, and the memories it evoked?

Barbara popped the trunk open from the sedan's interior latch.

Dutifully, Tina scurried around the back of the car for her bags. Apparently trying to make a good impression.

"I can get those, Tina." Barbara rounded the car. Years on her own had cemented Barbara's preference for autonomy. Her loft in the city hadn't been grand, but she'd enjoyed having a place she could keep up on her own, without hired help. No maid, no need for a gardener.

It had been bad enough to lay off her small staff at the gallery she'd started in the city, only to close its doors for lack of patronage. Now, the last thing she wanted was to be waited upon hand and foot at home, especially by someone close to her age. All of thirty now, Tina would have graduated high school only a year ahead of her, if Tina hadn't dropped out.

Tina fussed about, hoisting the heaviest of Barbara's suitcases. She draped a stuffed garment bag over her arm. "You must be tired from the road, Ms. Holbrook. I'll just run these up to your room. Help you get settled." She took Barbara's bags and started toward the door.

Barbara grabbed the smaller valise and her shoulder bag. Was she really moving back into this mansion? For now, she conceded. She scanned the looming structure as she made her way up the slate walk. It had always been incongruous with the modest valley town of Hinsdale. This place seemed more like a castle than a home, complete with a limestone turret at the corner.

As a little girl, she'd been achingly lonely there. How many hours had she spent in that tower? She'd blinked her flashlight out that window at the top like some captive princess, desperate for human contact.

A pang shot through her heart.

Jack.

Gone were the days when Jack Gurnsey would watch for her signal. When he'd come running over to shimmy up the tree to that window. Though he'd returned to his modest abode across the way to care for his much younger sister, Julia, Barbara had to face facts. Her childhood romance with Jack was long over.

Even calling what they had *a romance* seemed silly. They'd been school kids, bonding over mutual loneliness. Going off to boarding school, then separate colleges and grad schools had all but snuffed their fires out. The embers of their relationship that survived Jack settling in the city had flickered into smoke.

At least by the time she'd gotten her masters and relocated to the city herself.

And how humiliating to surprise Jack there, only to discover him dining with Charlotte Somers, from his high school class. Not that Barbara presumed any claim on Jack. Not that Charlotte didn't deserve his attentions. Jack had done nothing wrong in taking up with that small town schoolteacher. But never again would Barbara bank on such a sentimental notion. Only to have life slap her so soundly in the face.

At the time, she'd covered reasonably enough. Quickly, her sputtered idea of intending to start a gallery for fine antiques had blossomed into reality. Amazing how far she'd go to protect that obstinate pride of hers.

Before she'd known it, she'd rented a storefront, hired help to stock it, and opened her doors. Too bad it was a business few seemed to frequent. People admired the patina of her upscale offerings, sure. But they didn't want to pay for them. Not what those time-honored treasures were worth.

Thankfully, Jack had left the city long before Barbara's losses made it pointless to continue. And with Aunt Grace's passing—leaving her this sprawling property and the remainder of the Holbrook family fortune—shuttering her business and returning to Sunnycrest did make sense.

It also provided a good way to explain moving back to Hinsdale, having nothing whatsoever to do with the fact that Jack Gurnsey had resettled there.

No sooner than Barbara had passed through the massive double doors and into the marble-tiled foyer, Tina called from the upper landing. "Clean linens are on the bed."

"Thank you."

"And I've hung fresh towels, if you want a bath."

Barbara sighed as she started up the sweeping staircase. Aunt Grace lay in her final resting place beside her parents, out in the property's family cemetery. No one remained to warm these echoing halls. They rang with the long vanquished age of aristocracy.

Sunnycrest was hers.

For what it was worth.

Every eighteenth century oil painting, every elaborately carved headboard, bronze statue, and sterling place setting befitted royalty. And as much as she appreciated the value of all of those things, Barbara wanted no part of it.

By the light of a fire, David watched as his father strained to remove a strongbox from its hiding place in the cabin wall. Never in all his years had David opened that strongbox. He'd only seen Daddy crack its lid a time or two.

Daddy sat with the box by the fire. Piece-by-piece he removed an assortment of yellowed newspaper clippings, scanning them one-by-one before throwing each into the blaze. Finally, he closed the box. His whisper rang with profound regret. "Catherine, my love...I am still so very sorry."

What did Daddy mean? Daddy spoke so little of the past, even when David asked.

With curious strength, Daddy packed a few photographs into his large canvas duffel bag. David gathered up sheet music, melodies composed on the mountain.

"Only as much as we can carry, David."

David looked up. "I can carry it."

"Some of it," Daddy said. "But we'll need food and clothes. Get that other duffel bag from under my bunk."

Obediently, David crawled beneath his father's cot and pulled out a smaller bag. He brushed a net of cobwebs off it. "Daddy, where are we going?"

"Back, Son." Daddy rarely used more words when fewer would do.

"To the outpost, the one where you get our supplies?"

"No, the other way," Daddy said. "First to the little town in the valley."

Excitement welled in David. "My valley? With the silver river?"

A faint smile spread across his father's face. "Then beyond. Far beyond."

Affectionately, Daddy gazed at a small picture of a beautiful woman, plucked from between the pages of their family Bible.

David eyed him uncertainly. "Daddy, who is that?" He gestured toward the other photos Daddy painstakingly packed. "Who are all these people? You've never told me about any of them, except the little round one of my angel-mother, the one you keep in your pocket."

Daddy turned faraway eyes on him. "Oh, David. They are going to love you. But you shouldn't let them spoil you, Son. You need to be sure to remember. Remember everything I've taught you." And with that his father took his violin and left the cabin.

David peered through the cabin window, out toward the crest. In the spill of moonlight, he made out the form of his father, as he took something out of his pocket. David's heart warmed. Every night this time, Daddy looked at that picture of his angel-mother. Then, he'd tuck it away and raise his violin. Daddy's melodies said so much. They were like poetry, drifting across a mountain breeze, resonating from the depths of his being. Tonight, sorrow poured from his strings.

If only one day, David could play like that.

The way Daddy played.

David's eyes filled. Why, he didn't exactly know. But for some reason, David ached inside. Daddy had said he should get some sleep, but David wasn't so sure that he could. Not with the thought of saying goodbye to everything they had known there. And not with the anticipation of the adventure ahead, come morning.

As long as it took David to nod off, morning still dawned quickly. Sunrays filtered through the cabin windows, bidding him to wake. He yawned groggily as he surveyed the nearly bare cabin. The canvas bags rested by the door, alongside their violin cases.

"Up, Son." Daddy seemed much better. "It's a long walk before we can get to a train."

David's eyes widened. He hopped up and pulled on his clothes. "A train... You mean it? We're really going to ride a train?"

"That's how we'll get you back to the world." Daddy picked up the larger duffel and motioned toward the rest. "Think you can carry those?"

David set the shoulder strap of the bag across his back and picked up their violin cases.

Already, it was time to go. Daddy stepped through the cabin door.

Something in David hesitated.

"Hurry, now." Daddy urged David outside.

"But, we'll come back..."

Wordlessly, Daddy closed the door.

"Daddy, let's not go. Let's stay."

Understanding read on Daddy's face. Still, he pointed to the valley below. "You see your silver river down there?"

David craned toward the valley. "Yes."

"You can't tell it from here, but there's life in it," Daddy said. "That's why it sparkles the way it does. Always moving, traveling on, reflecting the light. That's what we're going to do, David. And we're going to take our home inside us."

Daddy tapped his walking stick against the earth with each step as he led David down the slope to the east. After a last longing look at their mountain home, David followed his father.

Never had they ventured far from that summit. Even when Daddy went down to the trading post for supplies, he'd always gone alone. What the new day held in store, David couldn't say. His pulse pounded inside him.

Was that fear?

Or maybe just excitement about all that lay ahead? Daddy was right about one thing. The little cabin didn't seem so much like home once they had left it.

MORE AND MORE AS THE DAY wore on, Daddy had to force himself down the footpath. As best he could, David tried to get Daddy's mind off of his pain. They couldn't stop to play all their surroundings inspired on their violins, but David still reveled in the beauty of it all.

Soon, the footpath gave way to a trail. Every step of it a first for David. Every sight a new curiosity.

A squirrel reclined in their way. Gently, David nudged the creature with the toe of his boot. "I think he's asleep."

Daddy took a closer look. "He seems to be dead, actually. Like that hawk we found last month."

"Yes, I remember." David followed his father. "But really... What does it mean—to be dead?"

"It means the squirrel, the real squirrel under the fur, has gone away."

"Where?"

"There's a parable that says it's like going to a far country."

David glanced over his shoulder. "Will the squirrel come back?"

"No." The notion didn't seem to bother Daddy.

"Did he want to go?"

A soft smile spread across Daddy's cheeks. "We'll hope so."

Once more, David looked back. "But he left his coat behind him. Doesn't he need that?"

"No," Daddy said. "Or he'd have taken it with him."

Not so very long later, Daddy said they could stop for lunch. He'd packed fresh cornbread from their skillet and honey from their hives. They knelt down to the little brook they'd been following to drink.

An idea struck David as he watched the water tumble over smooth stones. About the squirrel on the trail. Why hadn't he thought about that before? "Oh, Daddy..." he said, "I know how it is, about being dead."

Daddy looked surprised. "Do you, now?"

"Yes, Daddy. It's like the brook, you know, that's going to a far country and it isn't coming back. And it's leaving little things behind it doesn't need, like the squirrel left his coat. He can go without it."

Daddy nodded. "That's right."

David leaned close to the water to listen, its sound dancing in his ears. "And it's singing. Can you hear that? It's singing as it goes."

A grimace pinched Daddy's face as he rose. He picked up the large duffel bag, straining under its weight. "We should keep going, Son. Long as we have light."

Again David followed, through the afternoon and into the evening. Till they made camp under the stars, by the warmth of a crackling fire.

As Daddy pulled their blanket over them, David searched the heavens. So many stars, more that he could possibly count, twinkled high above. "Do people like you and me die, Daddy? Do they go to the far country?"

"In time," Daddy replied. "To a far country, ruled over by a Great King."

David took it all in. If Daddy said it, it must be true. "But they sing as they go, don't they? Like the little brook."

Daddy rolled over and closed his eyes. "Yes, David. I suppose there are those who do."

Barbara removed her earpiece and set it down on the nightstand beside her cell. A full day of unpacking and setting things up had done little to make her feel at home. Literally hours on the phone.

Over and over, she'd had to repeat the same thing. All without letting grief get the best of her.

Her Aunt Grace had passed. Everything had to be transferred into Barbara's name. Yes, the death certificates had been sent. Like her dear Aunt Grace's life had been reduced to a pile of bookkeeping.

She stretched to her legs and went to the window. No matter how fresh her loss, something about standing in that turret always soothed her. Stunning, that harvest moon there. It shone down among the oaks and pines, illuminating the Gurnsey's wood-frame house, across the creek.

Warm lights glowed in their front windows. Like always. Only the place belonged to Jack now. So strange to have come full circle with him. Geographically. The thought comforted and tortured Barbara, all at the same time.

Had Jack really returned there to take care of his younger sister, Julia? Or had it been to be closer to Julia's schoolteacher, Charlotte Somers?

Either way, it wouldn't be long before they'd cross paths. In a town this small there'd be no avoiding the inevitable. Especially since she'd agreed to take over the remainder of Aunt Grace's term on the town council. No doubt, she'd see Jack there the first time they called a meeting. Charlotte, too, in all probability.

Incredibly awkward.

What should she even say to Jack after all this time? Hard to know. Maybe she'd better pretend he'd meant nothing to her, just as she'd done in the city. A year, they'd lived only blocks away from each other downtown. And they'd barely said two words. Nothing of substance, anyway. The few times they'd accidentally crossed paths, they'd made vapid small talk. They'd said how crazy busy they were, each with their respective lives. They'd mentioned they should make a point to get together.

But they never did.

Tina tapped at the doorjamb behind her. All day, she'd been there, polishing the silver. "Ms. Holbrook?"

Barbara turned. "How about if we make a deal? I won't call you Ms. Glaspell, if you'll stop calling me Ms. Holbrook."

Tina shifted to one side, her brow furrowed. "Should I call you Ms. Barbara, then?"

Barbara shook her head as she wandered back into the room. "Look, I... Really, I appreciate the respect you're trying to show me as an employer, but I like to think of us as contemporaries. Just Barbara is fine. If my calling you Tina is okay with you."

Tina's stance loosened. "All right, then. No hurry. I just wanted you to know that I have a little supper ready, for whenever you are."

"Is that Brunswick Stew I smell on the stove?"

"Your Aunt Grace's recipe. I hoped it'd make you feel more at home."

Unexpected tears pooled in Barbara's eyes. She averted her gaze.

"I'm sorry," Tina said. "Did I do the wrong thing?"

"No, Tina. You did exactly the right thing. I just miss her, that's all." Barbara steadied herself. "Why don't you give me a few minutes to freshen up, then we can have a bowl together."

"Nice of you to offer, Ms...I mean, Barbara. But I really need to get home. Got to feed Betsy and Joe. Get my own chores done."

"Of course." Heat prickled up Barbara's neck. How could she have been so completely insensitive? "I'll be fine serving myself, Tina. So, you can go on home now if you like."

"You're sure?"

"I'm sure, Tina. Don't give it another thought."

Relief crossed Tina's face. "I'll see you in the morning, then." She loosened the ties on her apron as she headed toward the staircase.

Barbara watched Tina go, all the way down to the foyer. The thud of the heavy door closing behind Tina echoed across the vaulted ceiling. What had Barbara been thinking, supposing that Tina had nothing better to do than to while away the evening, noshing on stew with her employer? Tina had her own responsibilities, like kids to feed. She wasn't at Sunnycrest as a friend. Tina needed the money.

Mentally, Barbara sifted through the list of friends she'd grown up with in Hinsdale. To call most of them friends seemed an exaggeration. They were just acquaintances, really. People who had nothing more in common than the town of their birth.

Almost no one had stayed. Most had gone their separate ways for college. They'd settled far and wide, well outside the backwater borders of small town life. Anybody who had anything going professionally had made their way in more urban settings, like she'd attempted to do. As far as she knew, only Charlotte and Jack had returned.

Jack Gurnsey.

His face flashed in her mind. That full head of tawny hair, those warm, cinnamon brown eyes. Barbara shook the memory off. She had to stop going there. Obviously, he had. And like it or not, she needed to face facts. Anything else would be borderline pathetic. Just like in the city, she was on her own.

In a way, Barbara preferred the privacy that came as Tina's rusty compact puttered away down her lane. But solitude sharpened that two-edged sword. That fine line between peace and loneliness sliced into the depths of Barbara's heart.

Once again, she found herself utterly alone.

A new day dawned. David doused what little remained of their campfire, till the golden embers vanished into a rising wisp of smoke.

Daddy bent to pick up his bag, then must have thought better of it. Instead, he stashed it behind a fallen log. "I believe I won't carry this after all. And we can get down to the valley quicker without it."

"But isn't our music in there?"

"Those are just papers, David. Our music, it's in here." Daddy patted his chest and set off down the path.

The farther they went that day and into the afternoon, the more the trail widened. And the more Daddy showed the strain of the journey.

Dusk fell by the time they reached a grass-grown dirt road. Little traveled, but a road. David marveled at the wheel tracks, worn into ruts. "Cars."

"Indeed," Daddy said. "Jeeps and trucks, too. From the size of those treads."

After a while, the dirt road intersected with a paved one. And it wasn't long before an eighteen-wheeler blasted by. Amazing. David had read about them, but it was quite something else to witness. "Did you see that, Daddy? Have you ever seen something so—"

David stopped. His heart ached to watch his father struggle to continue. "Daddy...?"

Every step seemed an effort for Daddy. Breaths came in wheezy gasps. Still, Daddy's eyes remained fixed on the road ahead. He pushed himself onward. A car passed, but this time, David hardly noticed, intent on his father's faltering gait.

Daddy stumbled with his next step and fell to the ground.

"Daddy!" David quickly stooped at his father's side. A truck rumbled toward them on the road. Frantically, David waved for help.

The driver slowed as he neared them. A leathery arm propped on the window frame told of hard work. Faded lettering around a painted ear of corn on the door read: SIMEON HOLLY'S SILVER QUEEN. But the man never brought his vehicle to a stop. He just shook his head at them and muttered. "Get a job...stinkin' lush."

David lunged toward the truck. "Please, Sir. Could you—"

The man revved his engine and left them in a cloud of exhaust.

David watched the truck go, completely bewildered. "Daddy, why didn't that man stop?"

Daddy beckoned David closer. "Nevermind, David. It's... Come here."

David stooped at his father's side.

Shakily, Daddy began to empty his pockets. Out came his old pocket watch and a worn burlap sack. With shaking hands, Daddy poured out the sack's contents. Dozens and dozens of shiny gold coins jangled to the ground. "Take them," Daddy urged. "They were my father's. And his before. Hide them. Keep them, David. Until you...need them."

David ran his fingers over the coins. "But, Daddy. What are these?"

"David, take them... Go on. I can't."

With a blink, David balked. "I'm not going without you. I don't even know the way."

The low rumble of an engine signaled another auto's approach. Worry traced across Daddy's brow as a beat up sports car slowed. Daddy forced the gold into David's hands. "Hide them. Quickly."

As fast as he could, David tucked the gold coins into his pockets.

"Hurry," Daddy said. "Don't let them see."

Just as David managed to conceal the last of the gold, the car chugged up. Decorative painted flames accented a matte black base, as if blazing out from under the hood. Music blared from inside. A grungy guy's arm draped over the wheel.

His darkly clad female passenger groused at him as they stopped. "Turn it down, will you?"

"We're not picking them up." The guy hoisted a canned drink and took a swig.

The girl snarled at the driver. "It's just a kid, Jimmy! Just a little kid and his old man!" She leaned out the passenger window, yelling over the still-loud music. "You okay, Dude?"

"Fine." Somehow, Daddy mustered the strength to cover his condition. "Just needed to rest a bit."

The grungy guy swatted at the girl's arm. "Sometime today?"

"Ice off, Jimmy. Like you got someplace to be."

"Really." Daddy pushed himself up. "We're heading the other way. Into town."

"Okay, then," the girl said. "Be cool."

The girl settled back into her seat and barked at the guy. "All right. Go, already."

The guy finished off his drink and tossed the can out the window. "Whatever." He peeled out, his wheels spinning a cloud of dust behind him.

Daddy covered a furious cough. Harder than ever before. Crimson liquid ran through Daddy's fingers.

Blood.

Panic rose into David's throat. "Daddy, you're bleeding. What can we do to..." He scanned their surroundings. They were still such a long way from town. But there, not so far away, stood a white clapboard farmhouse. "There's a house, Daddy. I'll get help."

Weakly, Daddy looked at the farmhouse. Finally, he nodded, wiping the blood off his hand. He fished some paper out of another pocket and took out a pen. "Go..."

With all his might, David ran ahead. As he waited for another car to pass, he looked back. Shakily, Daddy sat up, writing something.

His heart pounding, David climbed the porch steps to the house and knocked on the front door. Anxiously, he glanced back toward his father. In the distance, Daddy continued to put his pen to paper.

The door creaked open, revealing a lanky, sour-faced woman. Quickly, David removed his cap. "Good evening, Lady. I'm David."

The woman looked him over skeptically. "Lady? The name's Grundle. Ada Grundle. And what do you want?"

He motioned toward the road. "My father, he's so tired he fell down back there, and we'd like very much to stay with you tonight. If you don't mind."

"Oh." She sniffed as she threw her head back. "You would."

David nodded. "Yes, please."

"Well..." She leaned against the doorjamb. "In case you hadn't noticed, this here ain't no motor motel."

Confusion clouded David. "I beg your pardon?"

"We don't take in no tramps." With that, Ada Grundle slammed the door.

So puzzling. David knocked again.

Once more, she opened the door. The look on her face was no less exasperated, but she seemed to be warming. "Look, kid, if you're hungry I'll give you some milk and day-old bread I got left. Go 'round to the back and I'll get it." Abruptly, she shut the door.

Everything in David wanted to refuse the woman. But with a look back to his father, he knew he couldn't.

David rounded the little house and stood by the back stoop. Though she hadn't offered them lodging, there would be food and drink to take to his father.

With a huff, Ada emerged. She thrust a plastic bag of rolls toward him and a half-drunk quart of milk. "Now, git!" she said, "Before my husband comes home and sees you."

As much as he hated to part with it, David pulled out one of Daddy's gold coins. It wouldn't be right not to offer the woman something in return. "Will you take this, to pay? Please, for the bread and milk?"

Ada began to shake her head. But as her eyes fell on the gold, she bent down closer. Angrily, she jerked up. "That's gold! Antique, too. Gotta be worth...well, who knows what!" Her expression tightened. "So, you're a thief, too, are ya?"

David shook his head. "No, Ma'am."

"A thief and a low-life tramp!" Ada said. "Well, I guess you don't need this, then!" She snatched the bread and milk back with a glare. "You better git, Boy! Git now, 'fore I call the sheriff on ya." With that, she hurried inside and threw the bolt.

Horrified, David backed away from the door. As fast as his legs would carry him, he ran back to his father. He had to get Daddy away from there, just as quickly as he could.

Daddy tucked his pen and papers away as David sprinted up, gasping. "Daddy, stand up, quick! We have to go!"

Trembling, Daddy struggled to his feet. "All right. Yes, we'll go. I feel better, now. I can walk."

David put his bag into the roadside ditch. "We don't really need this one either, do we?"

"Not really," Daddy said.

Relieved of that burden, David picked up their violin cases. He wrapped an arm around his father's back. "Lean on me, Daddy."

Daddy rested his arm on David's shoulders. Together, they began to limp along.

Steadily, David focused on a road sign. Seven miles to go. The bright orange sun sank over the horizon. More cars zoomed by, kicking up dust and gravel. How could they make it to town before nightfall? "Why won't anybody give us a ride?"

Daddy shuffled on. "Hard to know anyway with strangers. Who to trust. Not everyone is what they appear." He trudged another few steps. "Can't get into just anybody's car, either. Not always safe."

David tried to steady Daddy, shouldering as much weight as he could. Another car approached from behind them, headed in their direction. Would this person be any different than the others? With night falling, would the driver even stop at all?

Never had David's throat been so parched. Daddy must be thirsty, too. David swallowed as the shiny car slowed, then pulled up beside them.

With a mechanical hum pitched precisely at middle C, the car window slid down. A pleasant faced man, younger-looking than Daddy, leaned out. He seemed friendly, much more than anyone else so far. The crisp collar of a pale green dress shirt opened under a loosened tie. Going to town?"

Warily, David exchanged a look with his father. Should they get into this man's car? But given their circumstance, how could they not?

"I'm going most of the way there myself, so I could give you a lift." The man smiled invitingly. "My name's Jack. Jack Gurnsey."

Quite something for David to go from seeing his first automobile up close to climbing aboard and riding in one. All in one day.

And the fascinations with Jack Gurnsey's car? Endless. The windows and locks went up and down, all with the push of a button. A tiny screen with a colorful, electronic map glowed to the side of the wheel, tracking their progress toward town. The device even talked.

Inspiration struck. David leaned close to Daddy with a whisper. "I should play it." He reached for the latches on his violin case.

Daddy put a gently restraining hand over his.

"But you told me I should always—"

A shake of Daddy's head said it all. "Compose it in your mind."

David listened as a sprightly melody rose within, as full of surprises as the car itself, whipping past the dusky cornfields. The lights of town twinkled just ahead. A few outlying farms dotted the landscape.

Jack Gurnsey glanced back toward them in the mirror that hung on the glass. "You sure I can't take you all the way into town? Honest. It's no bother at all."

"Thank you," Daddy said, "but we can manage from here."

"That's Hinsdale," Jack said as he pulled over. "Straight ahead."

David peered toward town as the sedan crunched over the shoulder's gravel to a stop. He pointed Daddy toward the glowing street lamps of town. "Look, Daddy, it's the lights we see from home."

Jack craned around in his seat to face them. "This is my turn. I'm just around the north side, but it's not more than three quarters of a mile into town from here for you." With a harmonious thunk, their door locks popped open.

David helped his father out, then retrieved their violin cases.

Daddy leaned toward Jack Gurnsey, his speech barely audible. "Thank you."

"No trouble," Jack said. "The Streeters, they run a Bed & Breakfast on the town square if you need it. Just look for the big flowering tree. And tell

Bill Streeter that Jack Gurnsey says to give you the off-season rate."

"Yes, thank you, Sir." David fingered a gold piece from his pocket. Maybe they should pay for the ride. Or maybe not. After Ada Grundle's reaction, the last thing David wanted was to be branded a thief again. Quietly, he tucked the coin away.

As Jack pulled off and turned, David studied the remaining distance to town. "Do you think you can walk that far, Daddy? To those lights?"

Daddy wobbled, as if he might faint. Just getting out of the car and onto his feet seemed to have sapped every bit of strength he had left. Clearly, Daddy would not be able to make it into town, even from this short distance. So, why in the world had he refused Jack Gurnsey's offer to drive them all the way there?

Daddy fought to communicate. "You... You can go. Tomorrow," he said. "It's vital that..." Again, Daddy gasped. "Hope is always...there, David. Never forget."

Seeing his father struggle as never before, David glanced around. He spotted a farmhouse nearby, its lights burning inside. Several other houses flanked the road to town, just a bit farther away. David's gaze settled on a weathered barn, the nearest shelter of all. He pointed his father toward it. "There, Daddy. See that barn? We're just going there. We can stay there all night. You can rest."

Even then, David wondered if Daddy could make it. More than ever, Daddy leaned against him for support. They would get there, step-by-step.

They had to.

Simeon Holly sat on the porch of his farmhouse. Nice to finally put his feet up. Beside Simeon, his better half unwound a length of yarn, variegated in pastels. Another one of them baby caps she knitted every week.

He looked out into the darkened sky, toward the full moon. "Well, Ellen...don't look like we'll get a drop of that rain they predicted."

Ellen Holly looked up. "Maybe tomorrow."

He propped an elbow on the arm of his rocker. "How long you gonna keep knittin' them things, Ellen?"

"Long as babies have heads," Ellen answered.

Simeon let out a grunt. After thirty-eight years

of marriage, he knew her charitable streak well enough. "Now that Grace Holbrook is gone, I s'pose I'm payin' for all that yarn, too."

"I suppose." Ellen kept right on knitting, like his point had sailed right over her graying head.

A long note from a fiddle reached Simeon's ears.

Ellen stopped knitting. "What was that?"

Simeon fixed his eyes on their barn. Just what he needed after a hard day in the corn fields. Ellen always connected every fiddle she ever heard to their son, John. Even though John had left his fiddle in the closet when he took off long ago.

"Simeon! It's a violin. And it's coming from our barn."

With a huff, Simeon rose. "Got you a keen sense o' the obvious, woman." Quickly, he went inside and grabbed his flashlight, then tromped down the steps of the front porch.

"Simeon, what are you...?" Ellen stood. "Don't go. You...you don't know what's there."

"Fiddles are not played without hands, Ellen. Would you have us go to bed and leave a half-drunk, ungodly minstrel fella in possession of our barn?"

She returned a sheepish look.

"Tonight, on my way home, I passed a pretty pair of 'em, stumblin' by the roadside with two of them fiddle cases. Betcha a nickel that's who it is, too." Simeon tested out the high beam of the lantern-style flashlight. "Though how they got this far, I don't see. You think I want to leave my barn to them?"

"Well, no." Ellen set down her knitting. "I suppose not."

SIMEON SHINED HIS BEAM INTO the barn doorway as they passed through it. High in the loft, the fiddle played on, filling the night air with runs and trills and all manner of rollicking racket. Simeon paused. He raised a silencing palm. "Don't even say it, Ellen."

Ellen bit at her lip. The way she always did, whenever she got blue about John.

Simeon stalked up the narrow stairway to the loft. Ellen followed close at his heels. Not that he'd invited her.

Finally, the infernal fiddling stopped. Simeon's eyes fell on a man lying back on the hay, moonlight full on his face.

A whisper came from the shadows. "If you'll please be as still as you can, Sir. You see, he's just gotten to sleep. And he's so tired."

Ellen froze.

So, he'd been right. It was those two vagrants he'd passed, back the road a piece. Simeon strode toward the voice. "What in blazes are you two doin' in my barn!" He trained his beam on the boy's face.

The boy squinted at the flashlight. "Oh, please, Sir, if you would speak lower... I'm David and that's my father. We came in here to rest."

Simeon's gaze swept back to the motionless man on the hay. He stooped down, then pressed a cautious hand against the man's neck.

"Simeon...be careful," Ellen said.

He waved his wife off and whipped back to David. "What are you playin' a jig for then, at a time like this?"

David ping-ponged looks between them and his father. "He asked me to. He said if I played he could walk through the forests. He could hear the brook. And that the birds and the flowers—"

Simeon rose. "Lookee here, Boy. Where'd you come from?"

"From home, Sir."

Simeon scratched his head. "And where, may I be askin', is that?"

"Home, Sir," the boy repeated. "Where we live. On the mountain. Way up. Far toward the sky. It's up where there's such a big sky, too. Much nicer than it is down here."

This conversation had to be just as senseless as they came. Once again, Simeon would have to mop up other people's messes. Most likely at his own expense. Simeon turned to his wife. "Take the boy to the house. We're stuck with him tonight, I s'pose. I'll call Higgins. Hopefully, the whole problem will fall into his hands, now."

Ellen tipped her head toward the man with a questioning expression.

Simeon put his hands out. "Leave everything exactly as it is for Sheriff Wahl to check. The man's dead."

David's face turned up. "Dead?" Clearly, the boy's wheels turned. Something kind of like wonder glimmered in the boy's eyes. "Do you mean...he's gone on? Like the water in the brook. To the far country?"

For a moment, Simeon could only gawk in disbelief. What was with this kid? Looked like he'd have to spell things out. "Your father is dead, Child."

"And..." David's voice broke. "And he won't come back?" He looked at Ellen something pitiful, then sprang to his father's side. "But, he's here...right here." He stroked his father's face. "Daddy... Daddy, speak to me. Daddy, it's David."

Pathetic was what this was.

David drew back. He turned to Simeon, his eyes brimming. "He isn't coming back? He's gone?"

Simeon nodded. Finally the kid seemed to get it. Then again, maybe not.

Some kind of dazzlement filled David's face. "But, no. This isn't the father-part that matters. It's the other, the part they leave. He just left it behind, like the squirrel left its coat."

If Simeon hadn't seen it with his own eyes, he'd never have believed it. Right in front of them, the boy's face changed, lighting up with something he could only describe as joy.

What was this?

David leapt to his feet. "He asked me to play, so he could go singing, just like he said they did. And I helped him walk through the forests and he was hearing that song, just like the brook. Just listen to this."

In a flash, David set his violin back at his chin.

Music rippled into Simeon's stupefied ears. "Boy, stop that! Are you clean outta your mind?" He pointed out the barn door. "Go in the house with Mrs. Holly."

Dazed, David looked at the woman.

"It's all right, David," she said. "I'll show you."

At least, the kid obeyed. David took his violin and followed Ellen down the stairs.

Simeon glanced back at the man lying in the hay with a perturbed smirk. "Well, if this ain't just exactly what I need."

David followed Mrs. Holly through the back door, leading into their kitchen. It looked nothing at all like his kitchen back in the mountain cabin. For starters, pearly white appliances snugged up between painted cabinets. In contrast to his wood stove, everything looked electric, like the modern kitchens he'd only read about in books. Small blue numbers glowed on the back of the stove, blinking out the time.

Mrs. Holly gestured toward a table and chairs. "Would you like to sit down?"

David pulled out a chair and perched on it.

Mrs. Holly looked so completely unsettled, but at the same time, strangely moved. "Mrs. Holly. Are you sad...about my father?"

With a shake of her head, she wandered toward the kitchen window. "No, it's... Well, yes, but... There are just some...things." She lifted the glass cover off a raised cake plate. "You hungry, Dear?"

A rich aroma filled David's nostrils. His stomach begged for something to eat. But remembering Ada Grundle, he couldn't help but hesitate.

Mrs. Holly got a dish from the cabinet. "Never knew a boy in my life that didn't like chocolate cake." She pulled a knife out from a drawer.

As hard as David tried to contain it, his expression must have betrayed his longing. That or his growling stomach. Either way, he didn't stop her as she cut a large piece. A smile broke across his face at the size of it.

"I thought so." She put the piece of cake in front of him and handed him a fork and a paper napkin.

The cake looked almost too luscious to consume, but David stuck his fork in and took a first bite. Heaven. So rich and creamy on his tongue. He'd barely swallowed the first bite when he gobbled down another. "I've read about chocolate...and this is it? This is—"

"You mean to tell me a boy your age hasn't ever had chocolate?" she said.

"Not that I remember." He downed another fork full.

As he devoured the cake, he couldn't help noticing. Mrs. Holly never stopped watching him.

"What did you say your name was?" she asked.

"David."

"No..." She leaned against the counter. "I mean David what?"

"Just David." The dark chocolate icing melted in his mouth.

"Yes, David, that's your first name. But what's your last name? Like, my husband and I, we're Mr. and Mrs. Holly."

David wiped his lips. "I never had another name but David."

"Well," Mrs. Holly said, "what's your father's name?

"His name is Daddy."

Mrs. Holly moved closer. "No, his given name. Like he named you David."

David shrugged. "I never called him anything but Daddy. That's the only name I know." A wave of regret washed over him. Why hadn't he ever thought to ask? Now that Daddy had gone to the far country, there seemed no way to find out.

"I'm sorry, I didn't mean to..." She sat down at the kitchen table beside him. "Can you tell me more about where you live?"

Just the thought of home lifted David's spirit. "Way up on the mountain. So high I can see my silver river, and the lake it feeds every day."

Still, she looked so puzzled. "But you didn't live all alone."

"Oh, no. With my father." David scraped chocolate bits off the plate and ate them. "Before he...went away."

"No, no," Mrs. Holly replied. "I mean, were there other houses, but yours?"

"No, Ma'am."

"But your mother..." She smoothed the fringe on her woven placemat. "Where was she?"

"In my father's pocket."

Mrs. Holly's eyes widened. "In your father's pocket?"

David nodded. "My mother is an angel-mother and angel-mothers don't have anything except their pictures down here with us. That's what we have. And Daddy always carried her in his pocket."

She seemed to relax after that. A little. "But what did you do? Weren't you ever...lonesome?"

"Lonesome?"

"Didn't you miss things?" she went on. "You know...people, other houses, kids your age?"

"Well, how could I?" David said. "When I had my Daddy and my violin and all my deer and the whole great big woods to talk to me?"

Mrs. Holly drew back. She blinked her amber eyes at him questioningly. "Woods...to talk to you?"

"Yes, all the time," David replied. Living down in the valley, she must not understand. "There was the little brook. You know, after the squirrel that told me about being dead, and—"

"Child, what are you, anyway?" She looked so bewildered.

With a last lick of icing, he set down his fork. "Daddy says that I'm one little instrument in the Orchestra of Life. And that I should see to it that I'm always in tune."

"Yes, well..." She never finished her sentence. Abruptly, she rose from the table. "Bed, now. I think bed is the place for you to be."

Barbara Holbrook pulled back the quilt on the mahogany four-poster. Had life really come to this, returning to the very place she'd slept as a child?

She glanced at the clock. Barely nine-thirty at night and she had nothing better to do than retreat to her bed. Long ago, she'd learned to wait until sleep lured her there. But she'd rumbled around the old place long enough.

That quilt really was exquisite. Aunt Grace had pieced it together so lovingly. Not a machine stitch anywhere. Aunt Grace wouldn't have that. Every thread had been painstakingly added by hand. Softly colored calico rings intersected with milky-white muslin. Ironic that Aunt Grace had chosen this wedding ring pattern. Especially the way things turned out.

Aunt Grace had never married. A spinster, people had called her. So hard to believe that no man ever saw the depth in her hazel eyes, the character she exuded with each and every choice. And now, it seemed Barbara would follow in her Aunt Grace's footsteps, where matrimony entered the conversation.

How Aunt Grace survived that kind of solitude, Barbara didn't know. But perhaps she'd been lonely, too. Maybe having a niece like her to rear turned into more a blessing than a burden. Barbara could only hope that much.

She slipped between the freshly washed linens. So cool and inviting. Apparently, Tina changed them every day. And she'd have done all Barbara's clothes, too, if Barbara hadn't insisted she could take care of them herself.

A hard worker, that Tina Glaspell. And the only one at Aunt Grace's side when she passed. Even

Tina had little Betsy and Joe. Though there'd never been a husband. Quite the scandal around these conservative parts. Despite the liberal day and age. Probably the reason Aunt Grace took Tina on in the first place. Just like her to adopt the little family everyone else in town snubbed. But that was Aunt Grace. She'd given and given, until she finally gave out.

Barbara scanned the room, bathed in the indigo spill of moonlight. The shoes Aunt Grace had left to fill seemed far more daunting than Barbara often let herself contemplate.

Aunt Grace's example had been quiet. She never talked much about all the selfless things she did. But like the consistent waters of the stream that bordered Sunnycrest, she had left an undeniable impression.

A challenge, really.

An attack of smallness gripped Barbara's chest. As deeply as she admired Aunt Grace's generosity of spirit, Barbara had to admit the truth. In the privacy of her heart. The last thing she wanted was the kind of solitary life that her Aunt Grace had lived. And yet, her trajectory was clear.

History would repeat itself.

And there seemed nothing Barbara could do but hunker down and make the very best of it.

4

Tina Glaspell tightened the sash of her worn terry robe. One of these days, that robe would have to be replaced, but no time soon from that stack of bills on the counter. She set the last of the pans from dinner on its hook above the stove. Somehow, another day's work had gotten done.

Wearily, Tina shuffled through her living room. With all the yard-sale furnishings, her rented house sure stood worlds apart from the estate Barbara Holbrook inherited from her Aunt Grace. Tina sniffed. As downwardly mobile as Tina's relations were, there'd be nothing coming to her one day. Even if what remained of her kin hadn't disowned her long ago.

Tina stopped. What had she just accidentally kicked? That tricky spot in her back smarted as she stretched down to retrieve the culprit at her feet, a toy flute.

Joe. Sweet boy.

How could she fault a blind child for accidentally leaving his toy there in her path? Or young Betsy for not picking up after her little brother? Already Betsy had so much more responsibility than any girl should have at barely twelve. Most kids Betsy's age played with their friends in the afternoon. Instead, Betsy spent her free time watching out for her nine-year-old brother. And without the first complaint.

Tina made her way back toward the tiny room her children shared. Even though Joe couldn't see a blessed thing, most people wouldn't approve of the arrangement, with Betsy beginning to mature. But most people around this place weren't single parents, supporting two kids on a housekeeper's wages. In this economy, she should be grateful to keep a roof over their heads at all. Even in this sketchy part of town.

Tina cracked her kids' door and leaned in. She set the wooden flute down on the nightstand.

Betsy gave her brother, Joe, a pillow. "It was right there, Dopeyhead." She climbed to the upper bunk. "Can't you remember where you put nothin'?"

She reached for the switch on a foundling table lamp. "Night, now, Betsy. No more talkin'."

Joe pulled up his covers. "Night, Mama."

Tina turned off the light. "Night, Sweetnin'. Say your prayers, now. Both of you." She closed the door and headed toward her room.

A sharp rap sounded at the front door.

How she longed to call it a day and get off her aching feet.

That telltale knock repeated itself. His knock.

"*Lord, help me.*" Combing her fingers through her hair, Tina trudged back toward the front door. No secret who waited on the other side. Still, she peered through the peephole.

Luke Dowd.

Not so long ago, just the sight of that lanky frame made her heart race. With those sea green eyes and that full raven hair, Luke Dowd could sure turn a woman's head. Somehow, the guy knew exactly what to say. Well, at first he did. He'd tug at her heartstrings. He'd tell her she was pretty. That he'd take care of her and her kids. Everything she'd always longed to hear. Too bad it all went up in smoke and booze, come the light of day.

She unhooked the chain and cracked open the door, shielding herself behind it. "You can't come in, Luke. I just put the kids to bed."

Luke pushed the door open farther. He hooked an amorous arm around her waist and pulled Tina onto the stoop. "So... You come out."

Tina glanced down the dimly lit street. Not much happened around this small town, but when it did, people found out about it. No doubt her neighbors across the way were already at their windows, peering between the slats of their blinds, watching to see what she'd do. They'd call each other up, or text to gossip about the latest. Even some of the church women.

She tightened her robe across her chest. "I told you, Luke. I can't come out. Ain't half dressed."

Whiskey hung thick on Luke's breath. "You hear me complainin'?" He pulled her close and pressed his lips on hers, kissing her hungrily. Unwelcome stubble roughed against her skin.

Decisively, she pulled away. "Cut it out, Luke. I told you. I ain't doin' this no more." In one motion, she pushed him away, went inside, and soundly closed her door.

She covered her face with her hands. There was no use kidding herself about Luke. Not any longer. For a while, she'd thought he could change. That he could become the father her kids needed. Or worst case, another breadwinner.

But all Luke's promises to stay on the wagon had been broken. And re-promised. Then broken all over again. No use confronting the guy about his problem anymore. By morning, he wouldn't even remember coming over, much less anything that she'd said.

Tina secured the lock and chain and leaned against the door. She watched through the peephole as Luke stumbled down her stairs and into the street, slurring words she could only hope to heaven her children didn't hear.

How could she have been stupid enough to believe that man's boasts? He wasn't the knight in shining armor he'd made himself out to be. Not by a long shot.

Tina had to face facts. Not like she deserved better. And even if there were a man worth having out there, he'd turn tail and run from damaged goods like her.

Simeon Holly slapped at a mosquito. Varmints were thick as thieves this time of night. All the more reason to resent having to stand out there by his barn past bedtime.

He turned to his farmhand, Perry Larson. Never mattered how unpleasant the task Perry got called on to do, he shouldered it without a grumble. "Hated askin' you to come back out here when you're off, Perry."

"Don't mind a bit." The African-American man shot him a congenial smile. "Not like I have anybody to go home to," Perry said. "Wasn't doin' nothin' but playin' Rummy at the firehouse. And you know how that Luke Dowd cheats."

Cyrus Higgins descended the steps from the barn's loft. As town coroner, he'd been Simeon's first call. Even before the sheriff. Though Simeon wouldn't let that on to Bill Streeter when he got there. The portly pig farmer and land baron liked to think of himself as everybody's priority. No matter what went on around those parts.

Headlights swept the drive as Streeter motored up to the barn and climbed out of his SUV.

Higgins dusted bits of hay off his jacket. "Well, you called it right, Simeon. Dead is dead. Looks like it's been an hour or two. Like I told Sheriff Wahl, no sign of foul play. Natural causes, I'd venture."

Streeter waddled up with that duck-footed walk of his. "Been thinking about this, Holly. Technically, I still hold the note on this farm. I'll run the paperwork by Jack Gurnsey in the morning. But I'm guessing as the law sees it, that stiff up there is still your responsibility. The man died in your barn."

"He got there trespassing." Simeon had already told Streeter that when he'd called on the phone, but it bore repeating. "Plenty of signs posted out there, clear as day."

Streeter set chubby fists akimbo on his hips. "Sounds like a personal predicament to me."

Perry stepped between Simeon and Streeter. "All due respect, Streeter. I say the town should cover it." Perry gestured back toward Simeon. "He don't even know the man."

Higgins scratched at his neck. "Problem is, this town's got no budget for burying homeless."

"I can tell you right now," Simeon said. "I ain't payin' to bury him. I got bills."

"That you do." An uppity grin cracked Streeter's face. "Speaking of your note to me on this farm—it's due before you know it."

Perry scuffed his boot in the dirt. "Ain't none of us likely to forget what we owe you, Streeter."

Simeon dropped his head lest he let his tongue get the better of him. Truth be told, Streeter owned half the county. Long as Streeter had that note to hold over Simeon's head, he'd just have to grit his teeth and take whatever Streeter dished up.

Higgins gestured toward the loft. "So, given the natural circumstances, Sheriff Wahl gave us the go-ahead to remove the body."

Simeon started into the barn. "Might as well get this over with."

With the four of them working together, it didn't take long to get the man's body loaded into the back of Higgins' hearse.

Not that Streeter helped much.

Simeon wiped his hands on the sides of his pants. He'd have to wash, for sure, soon as he got inside. No tellin' what that man had been into.

Higgins latched the vehicle's rear hatch. "We'll call a meeting to deal with the particulars come morning. Meantime, I'll keep Sheriff Wahl in the loop, make sure we get things right."

Simeon motioned toward Perry. "Me an' Perry, we got corn to harvest come mornin'."

Streeter scowled. "An' I got hogs to slop. Had plans tonight, too, I might add."

Perry glanced back at the body in the hearse. "Somethin' tells me ain't none of us had a worse night than his."

Annoyed as he was, Simeon had to admit it. As usual, Perry was right.

Mrs. Holly led David into what looked like it was once a boy's room. Maybe even a boy close to David's age. A rag-wool rug on the floor led up to a four-poster bed, so high it had little wooden steps rising to it. Never had David seen such a grand bed, except in those picture books Daddy had shown him, back home on the mountain.

He watched as she opened a box from the top shelf of the closet and pulled out a pair of cotton pajamas. Carefully, she laid them out on the bed, sniffling back a tear. "These should fit."

David gazed around. Where was the boy who used to live in this room? He probably shouldn't ask. Not as sad as Mrs. Holly looked.

He checked around the room. A fishing rod rested on pegs, displayed on the wall. Next to it, a BB gun. Mounted after that hung a glassed-in case of bugs and moths, impaled on pins. David shuddered. Why would anyone hurt such amazing creatures, let alone put them on display?

Mrs. Holly retreated to the door. "Goodnight, then, David."

"Goodnight, Mrs. Holly."

She left quickly, drawing the door closed behind her.

David examined the set of striped pajamas she'd left. They smelled of cedar, like the trees by the stream. And it did feel good to change into something clean. Even if the pants legs needed to be rolled up shorter.

Voices sounded from outside, by the barn. David wandered to the window. More men. Mr. Holly stood out there with a few others by a long black car. A hollowness rolled in the pit of David's stomach. There were other people around, so why did he feel so completely alone?

David crossed the room. He pressed his fingers down into the terribly tall bed. So squishy compared to the cot his father built.

Daddy.

There'd never been a day when Daddy hadn't read him a story before they settled into bed. Or David had read to Daddy. They'd read every book on their shelves multiple times, from a wide range of classics like *Pilgrim's Progress, Ivanhoe, Les Miserables,* and *Robinson Crusoe,* to the epic adventures in their family *Bible*. But there would be no bedtime story tonight. No tucking under the covers. Not with Daddy gone to the far country.

Refusing the too-tall bed, David curled up on the round rag rug, then hugged his violin case close to his chest. He tried his best to stop them, but sobs racked through David. He wiped his eyes on the borrowed pajama sleeve.

If going to the far country were a good thing for Daddy, why did it make him hurt this way? And what was he to do, now that Daddy had gone? He couldn't get back to the mountain cabin. Not tonight. But maybe if he closed his eyes, there would be some peace in sleep. Perhaps he could dream of long ago times, before they left their mountain home.

David rubbed his eyes. So foggy, this night.

And his body. So small.

Like suddenly, he was only a small child again. Alone. But not at home on the mountain. Running as fast as he could through an imposing maze of skyscrapers.

A shadowy figure lumbered, shouting angrily after him. With such short legs, he could only escape so quickly. Footsteps slapped behind him on a rainy city street.

So many people, towering over him... He darted through passers by. Their distorted faces snarled at him, terrifying him all the more.

His pulse pounding, David ran as fast as he could. "Daddy!" he cried. Daddy would help if he were there. But Daddy was nowhere to be seen.

Exhausted, David slipped into an alley. There had to be somewhere to go. Someplace to hide.

Never had refuse provided such sweet refuge. David buried himself in garbage. With one hand, he pinched his nose to block out the stench. The other hand, David clamped over his mouth. Otherwise the scream crawling up his throat might rip right out and give his hiding place away.

David woke, heaving for air. Sweat soaked his pajamas. It had seemed so real, but no. It had been nothing more than a bad dream.

He didn't have that nightmare often. But whenever he did, Daddy had always been there to comfort him. To hold him tight and remind him it wasn't real. That he was safe.

David drew his violin case closer. Somehow, come morning, he had to get home.

5

David stirred. How did he get so stiff? He pushed back the edge of the rag rug he'd curled up over himself on the floor. "Daddy, where...?" Groggily, he gazed around the room.

Oh, yes.

The place where Mrs. Holly took him after Daddy went to the far country. That's where he'd slept.

He scrambled to his feet and made his way to the window. The sun cast golden beams over the treetops. A new day. Just like always. But somehow, everything seemed different.

Below, across the yard, Mr. Holly's barn doors swung open. A man with warm brown skin latched them into place, then walked away. Who could that be?

As quickly as he could, David slipped out of John Holly's old pajamas and thrust on his own clothes. The hidden gold jingled in his pockets. A few coins popped all the way out and rolled noisily onto the wood floor. "Shhh!" What would Mr. and Mrs. Holly think of him if they caught him with all that gold? Fitfully, David put the gold pieces back into Daddy's burlap sack, nestled inside a handkerchief. Maybe that would silence them. He stuffed the sack deep into his inside jacket pocket and buttoned it shut.

His violin case in tow, David tiptoed into the hall, then down the stairs. Clanking sounded from the kitchen. Probably Mrs. Holly. Quietly, he stole out toward the barn.

The place he'd left Daddy.

Rung by rung, David climbed the ladder to the loft. Reaching the top, he scanned the hay-covered floor. Nothing. Where could Daddy be?

A baritone voice resonated. "So, you're the boy, are you?"

Startled, David whipped around.

The brown-skinned man stepped out from behind a stack of hay bales, a pitchfork in his hand, towering over David.

Never had David laid eyes on a person like this before. He studied the man with curious awe.

"Didn't ya ever seen no black man before?" the man asked.

"No, Sir. Not in real life," David said. "Only in books. About men who did wonderful things. Like Frederick Douglass and George Washington Carver. Oh, yes. And writers like Langston Hughes."

The man shuffled his foot in the hay. "Well, I don't suppose I'm near the ranks of them, but... My name's Larson. Perry Larson. I work for Mr. Holly, here on his farm."

David turned back toward where his father had stretched out to rest in the loft. Maybe this Perry Larson could help. "Oh, Sir, please...where is he? My daddy. I mean the part he left behind him. The part like the fur coat."

The man scrunched his face. "Fur coat? I didn't see no fur coat. You best be talkin' to Mr. Holly 'bout that."

"Where is Mr. Holly?"

Perry Larson motioned through the loft's window. "Out in the cornfields right now, gettin' the day's work goin'. But you can watch for him, there from the porch. He'll be along for breakfast right soon."

PERCHED ON THE PORCH STEPS, David drank in the view of the distant mountains. Hard to tell which one was their mountain from this point-of-view. Maybe it'd be easier to recognize from a bit closer.

A bright green caterpillar inched along the rail. So interesting, the way it moved. Where did that creature think it was going? David set his finger in the caterpillar's path and it climbed right on board. A friend.

Actually, this caterpillar might feel just as alone as David did. "You don't want to be here either, do you? Not later anyway. Not when you sprout those wings you're going to have."

As the caterpillar moved onto David's other hand, the impaled insects in the case upstairs flashed through his mind. "And you sure won't want to be here when you see what they do to..." David shuddered. "Just stay away from anybody with pins, okay?"

Longingly, David looked toward home. "See that mountain? That's where you should fly off to one day. There are trees all around and flowers and birds." David paused. "Well, you should probably stay away from birds, too."

Gently, David put the caterpillar back on the rail. Once more, he turned toward his mountain, a decision forming.

He picked up his violin case and headed toward the road.

Not long after he set off, David's stomach growled. The taste of Mrs. Holly's chocolate cake drifted through his memory. Maybe she would have given him more if he'd stayed for breakfast. But then again, once he got back to the mountain, he could find some ripe berries, the ones Daddy taught him were safe to eat. Those wild blackberries they'd found on the way down would be good. Made his mouth water, just at the thought.

David stopped at an intersection. Making the trek had seemed a good idea when he'd set off, but now... The farther David had walked, the more his recollection blurred. Which was the right way to get there? Jack Gurnsey had taken a turn or two when he drove them in his car. Why hadn't David paid closer attention to the road, instead of all those gadgets?

David stared at the crossroads signs. Neither led directly to the mountains ahead. And a wrong choice could send him miles in the wrong direction.

Daddy would have known the way. But Daddy wasn't there.

So, what was David to do?

Barbara Holbrook opened her eyes. Morning light filtered in through the crack in the drapes, dust particles suspended on slender rays. She stretched for the ringing phone.

Not even nine o'clock. Who would call before nine? This far away from the city, she'd have to reacclimate to farmer's hours. "Hello?"

"Morning, Miss Holbrook. Bill Streeter, here. I heard that you blew back into town." Streeter's boisterous voice blared through her receiver. Hadn't anyone ever told the man he didn't need to speak at that level to be heard?

"Yes, Mr. Streeter. Is there something I can do for you?" She could only hope there wasn't.

"Matter of fact, indeed there is. I've called an emergency council meeting, here in a bit."

"Define *a bit*," Barbara replied.

"Oh, an hour or so."

Barbara checked the clock as she sat up. "At ten?"

"Ten-thirty. Now, don't you worry your pretty head, there Little Missy," he said. "We know you've got plenty to occupy yourself out there at Sunnycrest, without gettin' all wrapped up in this town's business."

Hmph. Her gaze narrowed. "What kind of business?"

"Look, we get that you're not up to speed," Streeter replied. "I'm just doin' diligence. By-laws say that, technically, I have to notify you. Give you a chance to show, since you're fillin' your late Aunt Grace's seat. Course, that's only a formality. Just till the next vote."

Small town politics held little attraction for Barbara. Especially when she'd planned to take the whole day to sort out more of Aunt Grace's affairs. But something in Streeter's smarmy presumption irked Barbara. "Actually, I'm glad you called, Mr. Streeter. I think I'd like to come."

"No need to push yourself, Little Lady. I know you women need your beauty sleep. Time to do your hair. Put on your face, paint your nails, and what all."

Steam rose inside Barbara. "The timing is no problem, Mr. Streeter. I'll see you there." Quickly, she hung up. Before the man had a chance to patronize her more than he already had.

Aunt Grace hadn't been a backbiter. But without telling tales, she'd made her desire for Barbara to assume her vacated council seat patently clear. All Barbara could figure was, Aunt Grace must have had her reasons. Maybe to keep Streeter's iron fist on the town in check. Or maybe, if she knew Aunt Grace's wily side, it was that and something more.

Sitting on the town council would force Barbara outside the stone walls of Sunnycrest. It would bring her into the life of the town and its citizens. Aunt Grace never said it in so many words, but her subtext had been clear. No doubt, she'd had a particular citizen in mind. Jack Gurnsey already held a seat on that council, ever since his return. Going there would mean facing Jack, right off the bat. Probably that schoolteacher he'd taken up with, too.

Simeon Holly sat at the kitchen table across from Perry Larson. He turned to the weather report section of the daily paper. "Looks like another string of giddy ole sunny days, Perry. So much for all the preacher's prayin'. Not a drop of the rain we need."

Ellen hummed softly as she dipped a thick slice of her homemade cinnamon raisin bread into a bowl of beaten eggs.

Simeon grunted. Not like they had French Toast any ordinary day of the week. Used to be Ellen reserved that dish for special occasions, like Christmas. Or Easter Sunday. John always asked for it on his birthday, but that had been years ago when he'd sat at their table. And longer still since she'd hummed. No question about it. Already, the woman had gotten her heart involved in something that she oughtn't.

She positioned the egg-soaked bread on a hot griddle. "Always loved the smell of this."

Perry sipped a mug of steaming coffee. "Sure smells great to me, too."

"No need to make a big deal over breakfast," Simeon said.

"Nothing special," Ellen replied. She placed another slice of bread in the bowl to soak.

Simeon furrowed his brow. "An' how long since you made that French Toast of yours?"

She shrugged. "Just felt like it."

Best nip this in the bud. "I'll say it once, Ellen. Don't let yourself go down that road. The boy's not stayin'."

Ellen absorbed it quietly. Like she probably felt like she had to. Not because he'd done anything to hold the reins on her longing. As long as they'd been married, Simeon could read that much. And the last thing she'd do was challenge his authority in front of Perry. "I'm going to fix a plate for David," she said.

Simeon folded his paper. "You'll do nothin' of the kind. You called the boy to breakfast loud and clear. He didn't so much as respect that with an answer. He's manipulatin' you, pure and simple."

"His father died," Ellen said. "He's grieving."

"Come on, Ellen." Simeon shook his head at Perry as he set a napkin in his lap. "Boy's also half 'round the bend. Did ya take note o' that?"

SOME VAGRANT KID SKIPPING BREAKFAST amounted to the least of Simeon Holly's concerns. More to the point this morning, his harvester refused to run, no matter how long Perry tinkered with it.

Perry wiped his brow as Higgins and Streeter got out of Streeter's car. "Thing's half shot to pieces."

"It'll do us for another crop," Simeon said. "Got to. Not a word to Streeter, though." He cocked his head toward his landlord and the approaching coroner.

Perry grinned. "Like I said, purrin' just like a kitten."

Streeter swaggered to Simeon's side. "So, Holly. You get anything outta the boy?"

Simeon rolled his eyes. "Nothin' near sane."

Higgins sidled up. "Well, I need to see the child. I've got a letter for him."

What was this? Simeon couldn't guess. "What do you mean, a letter?"

"Found it in his father's coat," Higgins said. "Addressed to 'My Boy, David.' So, I figured we'd best give it to him first, seeing as it's his. But, then I want to read it. See if it makes any more sense than the other one."

Perry looked up from his work on the harvester. "The other one?"

Streeter scratched that shiny spot at his crown. The one he usually tried to cover with that greasy comb-over. "Yes, there's another. I read it all but that scribble of a signature."

Higgins shook his head. "I couldn't make it out either. And I was hoping to, seeing as how the boy doesn't seem to know his name."

To Simeon, this whole kit and caboodle had gotten way out of hand. "Nigh on impossible gettin' any kind o' straight answer from him."

Perry chuckled as he went back to his tinkering. "I tell you what. That boy, David...he's some kinda checkerboard o' sense and nonsense. One minute he's talkin' sane like anybody, and the next he's goin' off about who knows what all."

Higgins pulled a letter out from his breast pocket. "This one here, it's the second letter. Seems the man intended this letter to go to whoever decides to take the boy on." He extended the folded paper toward Simeon.

"Well, don't look at me for that. I ain't got my glasses, Cyrus. You read it."

Higgins unfolded the page.

Streeter cleared some phlegm from his throat. "Not much to go on, anyways."

"All right, then," Higgins said. He focused on the paper and began to read aloud:

> *Now that the time has come when I must give David back to the world, I have set out for that purpose. But I am ill, very ill. And should Death have swifter feet than I, I must leave my task for others to complete. Deal gently with David. He knows only that which is good and beautiful. He knows nothing of sin or evil.*

What kind of flowered up gobbledy-goop was that? Simeon scowled. "That it? That's the whole confounded letter?"

Streeter pointed to the signature. "Except the scribble there."

"Can you make that out, Perry?" Simeon took the letter and showed it to his farmhand.

Perry studied the scrawl, then shook his head. "Got me."

"So, Higgins," Streeter said. "You find any money left on the body? Anything to cover costs?"

Higgins lowered the letter. "Pocket change. Nothin' to count."

"He had a fiddle didn't he?" Streeter asked. "That and the boy's might bring something."

"Maybe." Higgins folded the letter in half. "If there were a market for the things. But who'd buy 'em used here? Not a soul in town plays but Jack Gurnsey, and he's got one already. Probably couldn't afford it anyway, now that he's given up his practice."

Simeon rubbed his jaw. "There'll be nothin' to pay for no burial, I'm guessin'."

"Afraid not," Higgins said. "Looks like it's gonna be on the town."

Perry tinkered away at the engine. "Your tax dollars at work."

"Gotta get hold of somebody at county, too." Streeter hacked loudly. "See 'bout what to do with the boy. I'm already pullin' together an emergency town council this morning, see if they'll squeeze out somethin' to deal with the remains. Whoever the man was."

"Well, not that I'm gettin' my hopes up," Simeon said. "But I s'pose we should show that letter to the boy. Maybe he can read that sign off."

Showing the letter to David turned out a far sight easier said than done. He hadn't holed up in John's bedroom like they'd figured.

So, all four men looked high and low for the boy as discreetly as they could. That is, after Simeon urged them not to say anything to Ellen. He sure didn't need that wife of his wringing her hands over David's disappearance, going six kinds of sappy for nothing. Not with all the work Simeon had yet to do this morning.

Perry rounded the back corner of the barn.

Still no boy in sight.

Simeon stretched out his hands, then let them slap to his sides. "Well, he was here. Right on these porch steps."

"Not 'round back," Perry said. "Nowhere I see."

Simeon focused on the rail. There on the post crawled a bright green caterpillar. "Blasted vermin!" With a swipe of his hand, Simeon knocked the caterpillar to the ground, then squashed it soundly. "Won't be chompin' on my corn now, will ya?"

Just then, Ellen emerged from the house, a knowing look in her eyes. Great. Now Simeon would have to get into it with her.

"Mr. Higgins," Ellen said, "your wife just rang."

"My wife..."

"Her sister, Mollie, called to tell her that a little boy with a violin is at her house." Ellen cast a penetrating gaze at Simeon.

Streeter guffawed as he poked Simeon's arm. "You check your valuables, Holly? No telling what he made off with."

Simeon's expression hardened as he started up the steps. "Blast it all!"

Ellen set a hand on his back. "He didn't take anything, Simeon. He was just tryin' to go home."

Higgins gawked. "Boy that age? Hiking up into the mountains...by himself?"

"That's what he told Mollie." Ellen untied her apron. "She found him, crying something pitiful there at the crossroads near her house. Wasn't sure which way to go. She tried to get him to come back here, but he wouldn't."

Simeon's jaw tightened. "Well, I've had just about enough of this tail waggin' the dog. I'll get him here all right." He pointed inside. "Ellen, go back an' call Mollie. Tell her to tell the boy he's got a letter here. From his daddy."

That would get the boy to come. He'd high tail it back there lickety-split for that nothing of a letter, Simeon wagered.

Sure enough, not two minutes passed before Ellen returned to the porch from making the call.

"She tell him?" Simeon asked.

Ellen nodded. "Left half his breakfast. Tore out of there like a shot, headed here."

Perry set his hand on the rail. "I could run pick him up quick. Take the truck."

Simeon wagged his index finger. "Ain't nobody here chasin' after no runaway." He fixed his eyes on Ellen, underscoring his point.

Instead of accepting it right off, the way Ellen usually did, she just stood there, holding his gaze. She wouldn't outwardly defy him. Not in front of the men. But still, Simeon could tell. It took everything and more the woman could do to keep a civil hold on her tongue.

He'd seen that look a time or two before. Especially once John left. The woman was too fine a Christian to cause him much strife. Not directly. Outwardly, she'd surrender to his will, all right. But the disappointment on her face told the truth. It whispered that her heart wasn't in it.

And hadn't been for quite some time.

Finally, Simeon broke their little staring contest. Before so very long, the boy would be back. Ellen's mood would lift at the sight of him. She'd get her hopes stirred sky high all over again. Her mind would wander off to thoughts of keeping that crazy kid.

Once more, Simeon would have to be the bad guy. Just like he'd been with John. But somebody had to draw the line like that. Someone would have to straighten his back and stick up for what made sense. Someone would have to get them out of this mess. And that someone wouldn't be Ellen.

6

David burst out of Mollie Tate's screen door with his violin in tow. Down their wooden steps he hurried, before breaking into a run across the front yard.

Mrs. Tate shouted after him from her porch. "Remember, the Hollys' farm is left there at the sign, then straight for a couple of miles!"

Merrily, David waved back, never breaking stride, his heart bubbling over. As soon as he veered left at the corner, he sprinted into the straightaway. Two miles wouldn't take long. And the quicker he got back to the Hollys' farm, the sooner he could see what Daddy had written to him. So, he pumped his legs just as fast as they'd go.

Before long, David spotted some boys playing baseball in the road ahead. They looked like they could be about his age. Daddy had told him all about baseball. Any other day, David would have taken the time to stop and watch their game, and maybe talk to the other boys. But today wasn't any other day. Today, he had someplace to be.

David blasted right through the boys' game, just as a kid swung his bat, cracking a line drive toward the center of the road. Accidentally, David blocked the batter's path. "Sorry!"

"Hey!" The batter shouted after David. "What are you doin'?!"

David turned back. "I'm getting a letter from my father!" Even then, he kept a brisk pace, skipping along backward.

Another boy tagged the runner. "You're out, Eugene."

"No way!" Eugene said to the other boy. "That's interference an' you know it, Asa!" Angrily, Eugene pointed back at David. "I don't know who you think you are. But nobody messes with Eugene Streeter!"

David felt his eyes bug. No mistaking that look on Eugene Streeter's face. Eugene didn't like him. Not one bit. David spun around and picked up his pace. Daddy said people played baseball for fun. But it sure didn't seem like Eugene Streeter saw it anywhere near that way.

His violin case bobbing with each step, David kept running. Downhill, with the wind at his back, it almost felt like flying. Like sailing on a cloud-boat all the way back to the Hollys' farm.

As David neared, he could see Perry Larson standing tall, waving his arms high, welcoming him. "Would you look at you! You can haul, all right."

David careened into the circle of men, gulping for air. "Where is it, please? Mrs. Tate...she said you had a letter for me. From Daddy."

A man David had seen talking to Mr. Holly outside the barn pulled out the letter. "Indeed we do. This is Mr. Streeter, here. And I'm Mr. Higgins, the coroner. Here it is." Mr. Higgins extended the letter.

David savored the moment. He sat on the porch steps. The men seemed impatient, but David would not rush this golden opportunity to read Daddy's letter for the very first time. He would drink in every line. He'd think of how Daddy's voice sounded saying each and every word. He'd see Daddy's face, all over again.

Slowly, David devoured the letter, blinking back tears. An effervescent peace filled him as he finally looked up. "And Daddy...he wrote this to me? From the far country?"

"No, Sonny," Mr. Higgins said. "We found it on the... Your father left it for you. In his pocket."

"Oh." Disappointment blanketed David. "I'd hoped I'd heard since..." His chin dropped to his chest, till a sudden thought lifted within his spirit. "But it's almost the same as if he wrote it from the far country, isn't it? He left it for me. And he told me what to do."

Mr. Holly snapped his fingers. "Well, then let's have it, boy. Ain't got all day."

"You'll let us read it, huh?" Mr. Streeter asked.

David studied the taut smile on Mr. Streeter's round face. Could he be that boy, Eugene Streeter's daddy? That boy who'd yelled at him from the baseball game?

Just when David thought he might keep the letter to himself, Mrs. Holly came out the front door.

"David," she said, "I'm so glad you're back. Did you have a nice letter from your father? Mr. Higgins came all the way back to make sure you got it."

Something about the kindness in Mrs. Holly's voice made David's grip loosen on the letter. He held it out toward Mr. Higgins.

The coroner adjusted his glasses. "This one's a bit longer. Just signed "Daddy."

Perry Larson inched in. "So, what've we got?"

"Let's see, now..." Mr. Higgins read the letter aloud. But once again, it was Daddy's voice that David heard, every word transporting him to another place and time, every image springing into vivid life on the canvas of his mind:

David, my boy,

Though we've always been together, you are among new faces, surrounded by people who are strange to you. Some of them you will not understand. Some you may not like. But of one thing I am certain.

Hope awaits you in the world.

Do not fear, David, and do not plead to go back to the mountain. Remember this, my son: in your instrument lie so many of the comforts you long for. You have only to play, and the dear friends and comrades of your mountain forests will be all about you.

In the far country I wait for you, with the Great King and the Father of us all. Do not grieve, because that would grieve me. I won't be back, but some day you will come to me—your violin at your chin and the bow drawn across the strings—to greet me.

On that day, see that it tells me of the beautiful world you have left. Because it is a beautiful world, David.

Never forget that.

And if sometime you are tempted to think that it is not a beautiful world, just remember: you can make it beautiful, if you will.

Even after Mr. Higgins stopped reading, David continued to exult, his arms stretched wide and his face turned up to the heavens. Around and around, he spun, drinking in the encouragement of his father's words.

He slowed as the coroner's voice broke through.

"That's where it's just signed *Daddy*."

Mr. Streeter snatched the letter from Mr. Higgins. "That one's worse than the other." He thrust it toward Mr. Holly.

"Nothin' in it," Mr. Holly said. "Nothin' to help."

Perry Larson leaned over for a look. "I suppose I'll go fire up that harvester, earn my keep." He started toward the barn.

Mr. Holly thrust the letter back to Mr. Higgins. "Wouldn't you think if a man wrote anything at a time like this, he'd've wrote somethin' that had a speck o' sense to it?"

Respectfully, Mrs. Holly scanned the men's faces. "Well, you've all read his letter, now. Seems like we should give it back to David."

"Yes, well..." Mr. Higgins returned the letter to David. "Thank you."

As David tucked the letter away, Mr. Higgins pivoted to Mr. Holly. "How about it, Simeon? Can you take charge of the boy temporarily, till we get hold of social services?"

Mrs. Holly set a pleading hand on Mr. Holly's arm. "Simeon, please..."

Mr. Holly hung his head. "I suppose so, Ellen. Just for the time being."

"Oh, yes." Mrs. Holly's face broke into a smile. "Yes, Simeon. And he won't be a bit of trouble. You won't, David. Will you?"

David opened his mouth to speak, but Mr. Holly broke in.

"Won't be a bit of good, either. Otherwise, Streeter here would be speakin' for him to help out at his place, wouldn't you?"

Mr. Streeter pulled his pants up by the belt at the side. "Got my hands plenty full keepin' up with Eugene."

David took the name in. So, Eugene Streeter was Mr. Streeter's son after all.

A little ding sounded.

Mr. Streeter reached into his pocket and pulled out a small electronic device. He tapped it a couple of times. "Well, that's Jack Gurnsey. Looks like we'll have us a quorum at the council."

Recognition lit in David at the sound of Jack Gurnsey's name. Jack Gurnsey had picked them up. He'd driven them most the way into town in his car.

After another tap or two, Mr. Streeter stashed his device. "Of course, Barbara Holbrook flat insists on comin'. She'll probably make a meal of this. Guess we'd best head in, Higgins. You know how Charlotte Somers squawks if we start even half a second late."

Barbara rifled through her closet. She chewed at a thumbnail, surveying what she'd hung up from her suitcases. Everything had that crunched look to it. The kind of wrinkles that wouldn't hang out. Maybe she should have taken Tina up on that offer to do her laundry after all.

She buried her face in her palms. Really? In an infuriating way, Bill Streeter was right. She did want time to take a leisurely shower, to shampoo and style her hair before seeing Jack.

Perhaps to iron a dress.

Then again, maybe this would prove better. The last impression Barbara wanted to give Jack was that she'd get dolled up for him. The way she had that time in the city.

The hot flush of humiliation burned anew in her cheeks. Just like it had that night. When she'd spent hours primping for him. Only to find him dining out with Charlotte.

The fact that Jack had asked her to join them only made things worse. What? Was she supposed to be some third wheel on the date-crashing machine? No thanks.

Not like she blamed Charlotte. Jack Gurnsey may have sewn his wild oats in his teens. He may have gone the way of the world in college and law school. But something had changed in him since he lost his parents. Something in his eyes. Something that raised her hopes for more than the friendship they'd shared as children.

But now, it was too late.

She combed her fingers through her bed-mussed hair. No time to wash that mop. Then again, no point in throwing herself at a man who didn't see her.

Not the way she wanted to be seen.

With time ticking away, the no fuss route would have to do. She'd tie her auburn locks back into a plain ponytail. Wrinkled or not, she'd throw on any old thing. She'd march herself into that meeting with nothing more on her lips than a skiff of clear balm. She'd stand toe-to-toe with Bill Streeter, Charlotte

Somers, Jack Gurnsey, and anybody else who bothered to show.

No matter what anyone thought or said, Aunt Grace was counting on her. And whatever was going on in that emergency town council meeting, Barbara would make her aunt proud.

David leaned against the silver maple in the Hollys' side yard. Such a wonderful view of the misty mountains from there—across Mr. Holly's swaying cornfields—against that bright blue sky.

Everything had changed since Daddy's letter. Before, the mountains only brought confusion. Now, they anchored the horizon. Somehow, they steadied him, coaxing him onward and into the beautiful world.

Slowly, Mrs. Holly approached, a comforting expression on her face.

Mrs. Holly had already been nice, but even she looked different to him now. Like someone he could trust to help him along his way.

"It'll be easier now, Mrs. Holly."

She tipped her head to one side. "Why do you think so?"

David gazed beyond the mountains and into the heavens. "Just to know Daddy's waiting for me. In the far country. Just to know he wants me to stay."

"Yes." She took a few steps closer. "Does sound like that's what he wanted."

He focused into the distance. "Besides, I've got to stay, so I can find out about the beautiful world, you know? So I can tell him about it on my violin, when I go to the far country."

"You'll have to do that. One day."

David turned to her. "That's the way I used to do it back home on the mountain...how I'd tell him about things. Lots of days we'd go for a walk. Then, when we got home he'd have me tell him what I'd seen, with my violin." His eyes wandered back to Daddy's letter. Then, for whatever reason, Ada Grundle's accusations echoed in his mind. "Mrs. Holly... What is it to be a tramp?"

"A tramp?" She rolled up her sleeves. "Oh, uh... Well, just...a tramp. Never mind about that, David. I wouldn't think a thing of it."

"But what is a tramp?" David said. "Because a lady called me that, and if it's like a thief, then—"

"No, no, David. That's not what it means, not at all."

"Then, what is it?"

"Why, it's just..." She tucked a lock of hair behind her ear. "To tramp, you know, to...walk along the road. Like from one place to the other. And not to live in a house."

"Oh, just walking?" What a relief. "That's all right, then. I'd love to be a tramp and so would Daddy. We tramped lots of times in the summer. We didn't stay in the cabin hardly any. Just lived outside all day and night. And I never knew what the pine trees were saying till I heard them at night, lying underneath them."

Mrs. Holly's face went blank.

"You've heard them, haven't you?"

"At night?" she asked. "Pine trees?"

"Oh, haven't you heard them at night?" David flipped open the latches of his violin case. "Because if you've only heard them in the daytime, you can't tell what they really are. But I can tell you." He set his instrument to his chin. "Listen, now, Mrs. Holly. This is what they say."

His heart brimming, David plunged into a melody—not one he'd ever played before. Just the music that filled his spirit as he thought of those majestic mountain pines, swaying with the breeze, under a starlit sky. With his strings he described their red-brown bark, their refreshing scent, their far reaching branches, those long evergreen needles. And the pinecones he used to collect.

He could have gone on and on. And sometimes he did. But this song wasn't to keep to himself. This one was a gift for Mrs. Holly.

David lowered his bow and searched her face. "Do you understand?"

Mrs. Holly didn't say a word. She just nodded, barely, her lips slightly parted. Her amber eyes transfixed.

"You do understand. Don't you, Mrs. Holly?"

She patted a hand under her throat. "You know, David. I think I may be starting to."

Just then, Mr. Holly strode over. "Ellen, have you nothing better to do all day?"

She turned toward her husband, her face reddening. "Oh, yes. I have a million things." She brushed her fingers lightly across David's shoulder, then hurried toward the house.

Once again, David set his bow to the violin. Maybe he could help Mr. Holly understand, too. The rolling countryside filled his mind with inspiration.

"Look here, boy," Mr. Holly said. "Don't you do nothin' but fiddle?"

Abruptly, David stopped to look up at the farmer. "Well, I don't play all the time. I have to eat and sleep. And study."

Mr. Holly shook his head. "But did you ever do any useful labor, boy? Were you always so confounded idle?"

"Oh, I wasn't idle, Sir." David lowered his violin. "Daddy said I should never be idle. He said every instrument was needed in the great Orchestra of Life, and that if I didn't stay in tune...or if I didn't play my part—"

An exasperated huff shot from Mr. Holly's nose. "I mean, did he never set you to real work?"

"Work?" David mulled it over. Daddy's letter returned to his mind. "Oh, yes, Sir. He said I had a beautiful work to do and that hope was waiting for me out in the world. That's why we came down from the mountain."

"I'm talkin' about real work, Boy. Like, you see that pile of logs there?" The farmer pointed.

"Yes, Sir." To David, the pile seemed to be a staggering size. Much larger than he and Daddy ever kept.

"You know how to chop wood?" Mr. Holly asked. "Without cuttin' somethin' vital off?"

"I think so." To tell the truth, Daddy used to do all the chopping. David had just helped stack and carry the pieces. But he'd watched Daddy swing their axe plenty of times. He'd heard the crack of the wood as Daddy split each log into quarters.

David rose and followed Mr. Holly. Maybe chopping wood was part of that beautiful work Daddy said he would do in the world. No other way to find out than to lift Mr. Holly's axe and give the task a try.

7

Jack Gurnsey pushed through the double oak doors of Hinsdale's Town Hall. The peeling paint and ageing structure had certainly seen better days. Far from his chicly outfitted law offices in the city. But at minimum, his seat on the council provided him with a semblance of professional presence in town. Beyond handling the occasional real estate closing or foreclosure.

The usuals had already congregated. Cyrus Higgins, Bill Streeter, and Sheriff Wahl gabbed over sugar-glazed doughnuts. Horse rancher Buck Taylor poured a cup of coffee, then offered it to Charlotte. "Cup o' Joe, Miss Somers?"

As usual, Charlotte bristled. "How many ways do I have to say it, Buck? Some of us don't drink coffee."

"Then, don't." Buck took a jaunty swig and strode to his seat.

Jack shook his head. Why Charlotte couldn't go with the flow of normal chitchat, he'd never know. As smart as the schoolteacher appeared to be, social graces weren't so much her skill set. He'd tried to loosen her up when she'd visited him in the city. That she'd called him at all had seemed a bit of progress. Initially.

As it turned out, Charlotte wanted nothing more than his legal services, setting up her will. Anybody's guess why a single woman worried so about the disposition of her estate at the tender age of thirty. But Charlotte seemed a hard-wired worrier. And having her affairs in order offered some comfort.

When the others took their seats, Charlotte pulled out a chair to one side of Jack. "Is this taken?"

"No, that's fine." Jack scooted over to give her some room. "Good to see you, Charlotte."

With a half smile, Charlotte perched, her back straight as an arrow.

Higgins rapped his knuckles against the head of the table. "All right, Everyone. I know ya'll have plenty to do today, so let's hop to it. Long and short is, for those of you who haven't heard, a couple of homeless came through last night, a father and his ten-year-old son. And we've got us a little problem."

This emergency sounded familiar. Jack raised a hand. "Actually, I think I picked them up last night, gave them a ride toward town. They have violins?"

Streeter whipped around. "What in blazes you doin' pickin' up vagrants, Jack?"

Jack sat back. "Hey, just trying to be a good Samaritan."

"Really, Jack." Charlotte shuddered. "Do you not keep up with the news? Those people can be completely sick in the head. Dangerous. Never make eye contact. That's what I teach my students. It's the safest bet."

Little cause to debate such fine points with Charlotte. Not in this setting or anywhere else. Even knowing how dementia plagued Higgins' mother, Charlotte had no compunction about speaking her mind. And she rarely, if ever, changed it.

Higgins resumed. "Point is, the man up and died in Simeon Holly's barn. No identification, no money to speak of. Worse yet, the child doesn't even know his father's name. Or his own last name."

Jack turned as the Hall's double doors swung open. Though he fought not to let on, the woman who entered took his breath away.

Barbara.

Memories flooded back. Pictures of simpler times he'd better swallow in this company. But like a chalky pill that wouldn't quite go down, that phantom feeling caught in his throat.

Barbara approached the table. "I hope I'm not too late." She scanned for empty seats, her gaze sailing right past his.

Streeter muttered at Buck. "Just like that old aunt of hers was, always had to make something of an entrance."

Odd. To Jack, Grace Holbrook had about the humblest heart on God's green earth. Of course, could be the fact that her net worth far exceeded Streeter's that stuck in the pig farmer's craw.

Higgins shook Barbara's right hand firmly, then regarded the group. "I suppose most of you remember Barbara Holbrook. She's just moved back to take over her aunt's estate, there at Sunnycrest. She's assuming Grace's seat here on the council. Least till the next election cycle."

For a second Jack caught eyes with Barbara.

Instantly, she turned to the coffee urn. "Go right ahead. I'll catch up."

She'd made nothing of noticing Jack. But as hard as he tried to resist, he could barely take his eyes off her.

Sheriff Wahl swung in Jack's direction. "You get any idea who the dead man was, Jack? His name, if he had family?"

Jack heard the sheriff, but somehow the sight of Barbara delayed his response. Like trying to speak under water.

Buck Taylor's boot kicked at him under the table. "Get in the game, Jack-o."

Jack turned back to the group as Barbara crossed to the table.

For whatever reason, she rejected the empty seat on the other side of him, opting for the chair by Higgins around the end. Apparently, she'd keep shutting him out.

Just like she had in the city.

"No, uh..." Jack did his best to recover. "They didn't say much actually. The man didn't. And I hesitated to pry."

Buck stirred his coffee. "You ask me, the whole thing's hinky. What kind of man raises a boy all secret-like on a mountain, 'less he got something nasty to hide?"

"Could be," Higgins replied. "Jack, you got any way left to do a little checking?"

Jack faced the town's G.P., Dr. McBride. "Doc, can you get some samples off the body, just in case we need them?"

"Already done," the doctor confirmed.

Sheriff Wahl slid some papers to Jack. "Got the fingerprints, too. Maybe you could pull some strings higher up on this, since we've got no case. Not enough to pursue anyway."

"As for the orphan boy, David," Higgins went on, "He's with the Hollys for the time being. County's been called about placement, so that's in the works. Leaving us to deal with the father."

Streeter dumped a trio of sugar packs into his coffee. "I say we cremate him. Spread the ashes. Skip the burial."

Dr. McBride leaned over for a view toward Streeter. "No sooner than you do that, some kin pops out of nowhere saying you shouldn't have."

Everything in Jack's legal training urged him to agree. "I wouldn't chance it."

"Well," Higgins said, "the town plots are right pricey. I already checked with our cemetery and Walter's not in the mood to donate, especially given the questionable nature of the recipient."

Charlotte clicked her tongue. "Skinflint."

That got Buck riled. "Hey, I don't see you chippin' in."

Coolly, Barbara folded her hands in front of herself on the table. "Will this meeting by any chance be over if we manage to find a burial plot?"

Jack turned.

Streeter sputtered. "Leave it to a woman to over-simplify."

"Yes, Ms. Holbrook," Higgins replied. "That would do it."

In a flash, Barbara rose back to her feet to address them. Still just as lovely as ever. Same dark copper hair. Same sky blue eyes. Same tug on his heart.

"As you know," she said, "there's a small family cemetery on the edge of the property I've inherited. You can bury him there. The town covers the incidentals, and we can adjourn." For the first time she turned to Jack. "I'm sure Mr. Gurnsey can draw up the papers." Without waiting for a response, she left.

Jack sat back. Since when did Barbara call him Mr. Gurnsey? Impressive, yet baffling, this woman she'd become. So formal. Especially as much time as they'd spent together growing up there. Where had the ease they'd once enjoyed gone? And why hadn't she stayed long enough to say hello?

Sheriff Wahl waved a palm in front of Jack's face. "Yo. Jack. You still legal to do the paperwork?"

Jack shook off the image of Barbara's exit. "Yes, uh... Give me the weekend. I should be able to pull something together by Monday."

Sure. He could draft something. But formalizing all the legal details would require interacting with Barbara. And if he'd read her right, she wanted nothing at all to do with him. Once again, he'd have to tamp his interest in her down. He'd have to respect the discreet distance she seemed bent on maintaining.

WITH SO MANY BOILERPLATE AGREEMENTS on Jack's computer, preparing the paperwork for David's father's burial didn't take long. Strange that a life could be dispensed with so expeditiously. Fill in a few blanks and that would be that. The man who'd just ridden in the back seat of his car would vanish, as quickly as he'd come into their lives.

Getting Barbara to execute the document would be the hardest part. Not that it would take two seconds for her to date the thing and scratch out a signature. But just being there with her, reaching across the gaping chasm of their estrangement. That would prove awkward.

After a quick click, Jack's laser printer came to life. Like clockwork, it began to chug out the pages. Leaning back in his chair, he gazed through his bay window to an unavoidable view.

Sunnycrest. Barbara's inherited estate.

Situated on a hill with the creek running around it like a moat, Sunnycrest's stone facade and corner turret made it look more like a royal fortress than a single woman's home. On the map, Barbara's expansive estate lay so close to Jack's humble abode. Yet emotionally, the place couldn't seem more distant. Still, Jack found himself staring in something of a stupor, long after the printer spit out the final page.

"Hey, earth to Jack."

Jack swiveled.

There stood his ten-year-old sister and ward, Julia, her arms wrapped around a scrawny calico kitten. One she didn't bother to identify. "Miss Holbrook moved back to Sunnycrest, you know."

He retrieved his document from the printer. "I believe she prefers Ms. these days."

Julia stepped closer, clearing her throat dramatically. "Look what I found, Jack."

No collar. Must be a stray. Like they'd both been before their parents adopted them. "He doesn't have a tag, I see."

"She," Julia corrected. "I checked."

"Oh, well, then. She." He counted his pages. All there.

Julia scratched the cat's neck affectionately. "I know Mom and Dad never let me have a cat, since Mom was allergic. Sally—that's what I want to name her after Dad's sister with the hair she's dyed so many colors. Anyway, Sally doesn't have anybody to take care of her. The way you take care of me."

Jack mulled over Julia's request as he turned to the computer and loaded a website for missing and exploited children. Not that David struck him as either missing or exploited. It seemed a long shot, but maybe David's picture would be there. "You'd have to take responsibility. Flea baths, feedings. Whatever."

"I will." Julia raised a hand. "I promise. Lock, stock, and hairball."

He studied his curly-topped sister carefully, seeing past her doe-eyed plea to the orphaned child underneath. Why that plane crash had to claim the lives of people as good as their adoptive parents, he'd never understand.

Still, Julia had a wily way of batting her lashes. She knew how to angle for whatever she wanted.

Jack clicked his tongue. "You know, Julia. Let's just say I recognize this."

"What?"

"How about this blatant manipulation of my heightened sense of obligation as your guardian."

An impish grin cracked. "Yeah, I admit it. I'm working you."

"Yes, I know" he said, stroking the light stubble on his jaw. "But you can keep her."

David shielded his eyes. Perry Larson must have fixed the old harvester again. In the distance, Mr. Holly steered it through his cornfield. Countless ears of fresh corn bounced into the bin behind it.

That was Mr. Holly's work and—for today so far—this woodpile would be David's. He set up a log and swung the axe down, just like he'd seen Daddy do. It landed squarely on the log, giving it a good crack down the middle. After splitting the log into quarters, he carried the pieces to the woodpile. Most of the pile rose too high to reach and the lower end had tumbled out of place. Piece by piece, it would have to be restacked. Neatly, like Daddy had taught him.

Must have been a while since the wood got mislaid, because in moving the fallen pieces, David made a discovery. A myriad of creatures scurried about underneath, some crawling about on many legs. Beetles, centipedes, even an earthworm or two. Pillbugs huddled into roly-poly armored balls. David dashed toward the house. "Mrs. Holly!"

Mrs. Holly looked up from her dishes as David burst through the screen door to the kitchen.

Breathlessly, he tugged at her apron. "Mrs. Holly! Wait till you see."

"Well, gracious," she said.

"You have to come quick."

She dried her hands with a towel. "I saw you split the wood through the window."

"No, not that." David grabbed her free hand and pulled her out the door, toward the woodpile. "It's so great. You can't imagine!"

She trailed behind him. "All right, then."

Reaching the fallen end of the woodpile, David lifted the log again. Dozens of fascinating bugs squirmed underneath.

"Oh!" Mrs. Holly jumped back.

David beamed at her. "Did you ever think all these amazing creatures could be living under here?"

"Ugh!" She wrinkled her face. Without so much as a backward glance, she stomped back toward the house.

David looked after her, perplexed. "But, Mrs. Holly..."

She raised a hand to decline as she climbed the back steps and went inside.

Just then, a Tiger Swallowtail flitted by. "Oh, look at you!" David followed the butterfly to Mrs. Holly's pansies, edging her vegetable garden. He dropped straight to his knees. Gently, he lifted the velvety pansy petals. "Why, you're just like little people. You've got faces, don't you? And look at you. You're laughing at me."

A melody sprung from David's heart. Quickly, he grabbed his violin. His bow danced across the strings, bursting forth with musical descriptions. The song of each and every blossom rang out, from the deep plush purple petals to the azure blues to the sunny yellows along the outside edge.

Abruptly, Mr. Holly broke in. "Boy, what do you think you're doing? Do you have the attention span of a gnat?"

"Mr. Holly, I—"

"Well, Boy? Is this the way your daddy taught you to chop wood?"

"Oh no, Sir." David relaxed his bow. "Did you think that's what I was playing? Couldn't you tell? It's the flowers. Listen." Again, David began to play. Surely Mr. Holly could hear the difference in the lilting tune the pansies inspired.

Mr. Holly shot up a hand.

Right in the middle of his run, David stopped. "You mean, I'm not playing it right?"

"I mean," Mr. Holly said, "I asked you to be choppin' wood. Not diddling with no fiddle."

"I know, Sir." David rested his instrument. "And I started to chop the wood. But then I saw so many beautiful things, one after another, and I just had to play them. Don't you see?"

The farmer slung a look back toward the chopping block. "All I see is most a cord o' wood needin' split."

David rose. "You mean, even then I should have split some more wood first?"

Mr. Holly wiped his glistening forehead on his sleeve. "Should've given the woodpile least an hour or more, I'd say."

"But my song," David replied. "I'd have lost it. And Daddy always said when a song comes to me, I should play it right then. He said songs are like the mist. Or the rainbows, you know? And they don't stay long. You have to catch them quick. Before they go."

As clearly as David tried to explain it, the scowl never left Mr. Holly's face. "Boy, I don't know why I even try."

David's brow knitted. "Are you telling me I was out of tune?"

The farmer squinted. "Say what?"

"Out of tune," David repeated, "with the Orchestra of Life, you know. Daddy said—"

With a flick of his hand, Mr. Holly tromped away, muttering. "Don't mind me. I'm just the one who's got to put food on the table."

David watched him go. True enough, Mr. Holly worked hard. And if it weren't for him, David might not have a place to stay at all. Or chocolate cake to eat. Shame crept up David's spine. It snuffed out the song of his spirit.

His chin hanging low, David trudged back to the woodpile. He coaxed himself to set another log on the block, then picked up the axe. If staying in tune meant chopping wood—if that were his work for the next hour or more—then that's what he'd commit to do. With all his might, he sunk the axe into the log, splitting it with a satisfying crack.

For the rest of the day and all through supper, Mr. Holly's scolding rattled through David's mind. Finding that work Daddy said he should do might not be quite as easy as it had first seemed. Not with the world down here so different from the one he'd always known on the mountain.

Long after he'd been sent up to put on John Holly's loaned pajamas, voices continued in the kitchen. Maybe Mr. and Mrs. Holly thought he'd gone to sleep already. Or that he couldn't hear them down there talking. But with ears as sharp as his, David couldn't help listen. Especially when their muffled conversation repeatedly included his name.

Silently, David tiptoed down to the bottom of the staircase, to the landing just outside the kitchen.

"What are we s'posed to do with the boy?" He heard Mr. Holly say. "Doesn't look like anybody's speakin' up. Ain't nobody wants him."

"Shhh..." Mrs. Holly said. "What if he hears you?"

"Don't go shushin' me." He lowered his voice just a notch. "Point is, who's gonna want a child brought up like David was? Course, nobody wants him."

Tears sprang to David's eyes. If no one in the world wanted him, how could he live all those days and nights till he went to meet Daddy in the far country?

Mrs. Holly's chair scraped across the kitchen floor. Her rising shadow cut the light outside the kitchen.

With a start, David hurried back up the stairs.

"Hold on, Ellen," Mr. Holly said. "Where you goin'?"

"To put the child to bed proper," she replied.

As quickly as he could, David climbed the stairs, but not fast enough. Near the top, he heard the sound of Mrs. Holly's footsteps behind him.

"David...?"

He rushed inside the room and wiped his cheeks dry the best he could. A look in the mirror told him she'd know, as soon as she saw his splotchy red face. He couldn't hide how those terrible words stung. Over and over, they taunted. Nobody wanted him. Nobody. Wanted. Him.

With a turn of the knob, the door creaked back open. Mrs. Holly peered inside.

Just the sight of that caring face did it. Despite his best efforts to hold it back, David choked up, all the way from his belly.

Before he knew it, Mrs. Holly's arms were around him, holding him tight. Rocking him, like Daddy used to, after he'd had a bad dream.

She brushed a hand through his hair. "It's all right, Love."

But it wasn't all right. "Nobody wants me. Mr. Holly said that, so isn't it true?"

Mrs. Holly broke their embrace. She took a tissue from her pocket and blotted his face. "There now. It's true—he said that—and I'm so sorry you had to hear it. But there are two things you can know for sure. One, I always have tissues, for times just like this. And two... Let's just say, what's true for Mr. Holly... Well, it isn't necessarily so for everybody else."

"It isn't?"

She set her gaze on his. "If you want to hear what's true for me—I'm sure someone wants you. We'll just have to figure things out."

As earnestly as David knew how, he searched her face. "But Mrs. Holly, forget about everybody else. Do you...want me?"

Mrs. Holly blinked back tears of her own. "Oh, yes," she said. "And not just because you remind me of my son, John." She tucked a fresh hankie into the breast pocket of his pajama top. "Honestly, I can't say how things will work out. But Lord knows I want you, David. I really do."

A ROOSTER'S CROW STIRRED DAVID from slumber. He slipped out from under the rag rug and went to the window. Outside, past the branches of an oak, a sliver of the rising sun peeked over the horizon, painting the sky in pastels. Songbirds raised their voices.

A new day waited to be greeted.

The joy of being wanted filled David's spirit anew. He picked up his violin. The glories of this dawn simply had to be played. If not—just like Daddy always said—the rocks and the hills would cry out, before he led their chorus. They would sing of the new mercies born every morning.

Before long, David's door flew open. Mr. Holly stood there in his nightclothes, all puffy-faced. His hair stuck out wildly to one side. "Boy, what in thunder do you mean, fiddlin' at this hour?"

So much bubbled up that David couldn't help laughing. "Didn't you know what I meant? I thought the music would tell you. The rooster, he called to me first, saying, 'You're wanted, you're wanted.' Then the sun and the other birds sang the same thing, 'You're wanted, you're wanted.' And the tree tapped on my window to tell me again. So I had to get my violin right off and sing out that it's true."

"But it's Sunday, the Lord's day." Mr. Holly spat it, as if he didn't see the call to celebrate. "Did your father never tell you about God at all?"

"Oh, God?" Relief flooded David. "You mean, the Great King. Of course, Daddy did. He told me how He makes the sun come up. And how He wraps up the buds in their little brown blankets and covers their roots over because—"

Mr. Holly let out a huff. "I'm not talkin' 'bout no sunrise or brown blankets or roots. I'm sayin' this here is God's day. An' we don't start it off fiddlin' out the window or singin' with the birds or laughing' like no hyena."

David wrestled inside. "But those are good things. And beautiful things. Don't you think?"

"In their place, maybe," Mr. Holly said. "Not crack o' dawn Sunday morning."

He lowered his violin. "You mean, God wouldn't like those things?"

"Yes." Mr. Holly scrubbed a hand across his stubble. "I mean, no. I mean..." He pointed down the hall. "You'd best jump in that tub, right quick. Clean up good, now. Me and the Mrs... We're fixin' to take you to church."

Barbara splashed cool water on her face. Already, her first Sunday back had come, with all the dilemmas that it posed. Should she even go? Surely people would understand if she decided to wait another week or so before joining Hinsdale's congregation. But then again, staying home could send the wrong message.

No doubt, Jack would be there. Along with most the others from the council. But Sunday mornings weren't supposed to be about town politics, any more than dodging old flames.

Perhaps she could slip in at the last minute and avoid awkward chatter. Everyone meant well, sure. Though most had expressed their condolences about

Aunt Grace already, they'd repeat them all over again. Just as soon as they ran out of other awkward topics, like if she'd been dating.

This morning, she would take time to press something. That white linen blouse and those wheat colored slacks would look nice. Did the women of Hinsdale wear pants to church? She stopped. As long as she dressed respectably, what did it matter?

All the way there, Barbara coached herself. She imagined seeing Jack, chatting it up with Charlotte. Probably sitting with her—third row on the left, where the Gurnseys always sat. She could sit with Tina's family. Or maybe with Aunt Grace's friend, Ellen Holly. She never pried much.

Better yet, maybe she could find a spot behind the pillar near the back, where the view to Jack's seat would be blocked. If she got tempted to steal a glance at him, she could focus on that splendid old pipe organ up front. The one her great grandfather, Quincy Holbrook, had bequeathed there.

Barbara marveled as the service got started. Remarkably, things went every bit as she'd pictured. Except that Charlotte sat behind, not beside Jack. And someone else's attention to the organ eclipsed hers, as soon as the prelude began.

From the corner of her eye, she couldn't help but notice a young boy get up from his seat beside

Ellen Holly. Must be that orphaned boy they'd taken into their home—the one whose father she'd agreed to have buried at Sunnycrest.

Simeon Holly threw a stage whisper up the aisle. "Psst! David... David, come back." But the farmer's protests got lost in the enveloping opus.

Freely, the boy wandered to the front, all the way up the stairs to the organ. For minutes, David stood motionless, as if completely mesmerized. Only when the instrumental came to its soaring conclusion, did the boy approach the organist.

"Oh, please, Sir," David said. "Would you—could you teach me to do that?"

As amusement rippled through the church, Jack made his way up to the altar. He whispered something into the child's ear, then pointed him back to his seat.

The preacher taught after that, with no shortage of conviction. But the sermon that struck the deepest chord in Barbara didn't come from the pulpit. It came from that young boy, David. Clearly, he didn't care what anyone else thought, did, or said that day. He simply walked, unselfconsciously into the house of his Maker.

The way she only wished she could.

8

First thing Monday morning, Jack Gurnsey hiked toward Sunnycrest, a manila envelope tucked under his arm. Even on this bit of business, it seemed senseless to drive such a short distance. Besides, the fresh air might do him good. It could give him a chance to clear his head and reorganize his thoughts.

Before seeing her.

Nostalgically, Jack glanced at the overgrown path he used to take to the northern edge of the Holbrook property. The fallen log he'd walked to ford the creek had long rotted. And the sycamore he'd scaled from the ground to Barbara's window? That had been replaced with a statelier Norfolk Island Pine.

He had to shake those memories off. What point was there in entertaining his storybook childhood with Barbara, as if it had relevance in the present? Even long ago, when she'd welcomed his approach, they'd been little more than friends. As young as they'd been at the time, they'd never shared so much as a kiss.

Not that Jack preferred it that way. Especially the way she'd matured.

But that was neither here nor there. Barbara had made her preferences clear in their present situation. Who could blame her? Not like he had much of a career anymore. After all those years getting his law degree and passing the bar, the simultaneous deaths of his adoptive parents had left him with little reasonable choice. Abandoning the growing practice that had taken him on hadn't been easy. Especially since he'd barely paid off those whopping school loans.

But leaving Julia a ward of the state—that Jack couldn't do. And the only way to give Julia some semblance of a stable family-life had been to come home and give it to her himself. Even though she'd been adopted long after he was—maybe to occupy the place he'd left when he went to college. She was still his little sister. That was the least he owed their parents for taking the two of them under their wings the way they had.

Too bad the arrangement left Jack nothing to offer to a woman like Barbara. Not that the late Gurnseys had left them penniless. Julia's higher education would be covered in a trust. And between what they'd been left and the bits of legal work Jack picked up around Hinsdale and neighboring towns, they'd maintain a reasonable lifestyle.

Just nothing comparable to Barbara's.

Jack sighed. All too many men took advantage of women like Barbara, sponging off their wealth, contributing no meaningful effort of their own. Far too many sad divorces had crossed his desk in the city. Caused by gigolos who targeted lonely women far above their station. Only to bleed their victims dry.

Jack shook his head. No matter how thoughts of Barbara tugged at his heart, he would not be one of those men.

Not when Barbara deserved so much better.

Jack unlatched the iron gate and stepped under a rose-covered arbor into Sunnycrest's expansive courtyard. Deeply, he inhaled. As if somehow, the fragrant gardens would bolster his confidence.

Jack startled at a gruff man's voice. "Wouldn't have pegged you for a flower sniffer, Gurnsey." Jack whirled. What was Luke Dowd doing there with that unshaven face and those clothes that looked like they hadn't been changed in days? And those red-rimmed eyes of his? If he were sober now, he sure hadn't been that way long.

Luke propped his elbow on a shovel. "Tina's gettin' Barbara. Already knocked."

"Luke, what are you—"

"Don't get your back up, Jackster. I'm here to work. My girl, Tina...she got me the job diggin' that bum's grave."

"Oh," Jack said. "You using that shovel? No back hoe?"

Luke spat on the ground. "You think this cheap excuse for a town'd spring for a back hoe?"

Jack turned as the massive doors of Sunnycrest opened and Tina Glaspell stepped out. Apparently, Barbara had kept the single mother on staff, for the time being.

Not a moment later, Barbara emerged, simply yet elegantly attired as usual. As if she put little effort into her appearance. Interesting how much older Tina looked than Barbara did.

Tina sidled up to Luke. "Come on. I'll show you where."

Luke slung the shovel over his shoulder, barely missing Jack's head.

Jack ducked. Whether Luke or Barbara tilted him more off balance, he couldn't say. And why did his mouth have to be so dry? "Ms. Holbrook..."

Barbara nodded toward the manila envelope under Jack's arm. "I take it those are the papers."

"Yes. Yes, I..." Readily, he extended them to her. "Take some time. Overnight if you want to read them. I can come back."

A curt smile crossed her lips. "I'm sure they're in order."

"All the same," he replied. "I'd feel better about it if you had a chance to go through them. Make sure everything meets with your approval. You can give them to me tomorrow. When we're back to bury him."

Barbara brushed away a stray tendril that had escaped her ponytail. Once again, not a trace of makeup adorned her lovely face. "All right, then. Tomorrow."

Jack nodded. "In the morning. Yes."

She started to go, but nothing in Jack could pry himself away. He just stood there, ridiculously agape, grasping for something intelligent or thoughtful, to say. Maybe he should extend his condolences. About her Aunt Grace again. He'd spoken to her at the service. But maybe he should offer an ear now, if she ever needed one. Everything that ran through his mind seemed so impossibly trite. So greeting card standard. Nothing of what he really wanted to say. Whatever that was.

Barbara cocked her head to one side. "Was there something else?"

Finally, Jack dislodged his feet. He back-peddled a bit, nearly missing that step down from her door.. "No...I mean... For now, I guess I should sort of...monitor progress. Over there." He motioned toward Luke and Tina, on their way to the Holbrook family cemetery.

Her eyes widened warily. "By all means."

Good. Apparently, she'd appreciate it if he kept an eye on the proceedings.

Without another word, Jack headed down the slated path toward Sunnycrest's burial grounds. The very last thing he'd do would be to leave those two women alone. Not with Luke Dowd on the property.

More than a dozen stones marked Holbrook graves, encircled by a wrought iron fence, near an ivied rock wall at the edge of Sunnycrest. Jack made his way toward the far side where Luke had already begun to clear a spot to dig.

Tina stood a short distance away, twisting a strand of her hair, her eyes wandering toward the creek.

A certain reverence came over Jack as, one-by-one, he paced by Holbrook tombstones, dating back into the 1800s. Long before the Civil War, when sprawling estates like Sunnycrest had been far more plentiful. Two sons had perished at Gettysburg, before reaching the age of twenty. A weathered marker honored the passing of an infant, beloved though stillborn.

Generations of relations led up to the graves of Barbara's parents, Cynthia and Edwin, situated side-by-side. Finally, and newest of all, a modest brass plate marked the resting place of Barbara's Aunt Grace. Faith rose in Jack. No more than an outward shell remained under that blanketing sod. Not the way Aunt Grace believed. Of that, Jack was certain.

Quietly, Jack approached Tina. "I told Barbara I'd relieve you. So, you can get back to your work inside."

"Thanks." Readily, Tina headed back toward the house. From the looks of it, Tina seemed just as wary of Luke as Jack felt these days. Weird, since Luke had called her his girl and said she'd gotten him the job. Hard to believe he and Luke had hung out years ago. Or that they'd ever been friends.

Luke pitched a shovel-full of dirt off to one side of his growing hole, barely acknowledging Jack's presence. "I don't need supervisin', Jack."

Jack glanced back toward the house. "Just doing diligence."

Luke grunted. "Keepin' tabs on me. That's more like it." He pulled a flask from his pocket.

"You saying there's no need to?"

Luke wiped the sweat off his brow and downed a swig. "Been a long while since I seen a downtown drink like that Barbara Holbrook. All up close and personal. Like to have me some kind o' wild night with that." He hiked his brows lustily. "Wouldn't you?"

Steadily, Jack held his gaze. "You don't shock me, Luke." That hadn't been entirely true, but it still bore saying. If only to keep Luke from thinking he'd gotten under his skin.

"Oh, that's right," Luke said, stowing his flask. "You're Mr. Big City Attorney. Mr. I've Seen It All."

Jack kicked the brush aside at his feet. "Not any more. You know I've been back here most of two years."

"Well, don't sweat through your good suit, there, Pal." Luke gestured back toward the mansion, then sliced his shovel into the soil. "I know I got no chance with her kind, filthy rich as she is now. Woman don't respect a man that's got less money than her. And that there's a fact of life."

Something twisted in the pit of Jack's stomach. Not too often that he ever agreed with anything that came from Luke Dowd's mouth. But despite any wishful thinking to the contrary, this time he did.

Whether he liked it or not, life had situated Barbara Holbrook completely out of his league.

David wandered into the Hollys' living room. Mrs. Holly busied herself dusting a framed photo. Her rag slowed as she wiped it past the face of a young boy with a violin at his chin. Maybe this was the boy who used to live upstairs in the room with the too-tall bed, with the case of moths and bugs impaled on pins. "Is that your son?"

"Ah!" Mrs. Holly jumped. "David. I didn't hear you come in." She set a calming hand against her heart. "I thought you were still out there chopping wood. You seemed good at it, once you put your mind to it."

David dried his sweaty forehead with a sleeve. "Mr. Holly, he said it was enough chopping for today."

"Good. And yes, this is our son, John. From years ago. I suppose he was about your age then." She set the photo down and began to dust around a collection of knickknacks.

"So, John plays the violin, too?"

"Not anymore," she said. "I mean, as far as I know. He's more of a graphic artist. On the computer. Not that he got that mind for electronics from us. He humors me now and then with a hand-written letter." A sad smile crossed her lips as she continued to putter.

David counted down the row of objects yet to be dusted. "Are these things you've been doing all day, would you call them useful labor?"

"Useful?" She paused. "Who put that into your head?"

"Mr. Holly." David glanced at a vase of silk flowers on the coffee table.

Mechanically, Mrs. Holly kept cleaning. "Things have got to be done."

He gestured to the sunrays, streaming through the sheers. "But aren't you going to walk today?"

Mrs. Holly crinkled her nose. "To walk? Where?"

"Well," David said, "through the woods or the fields. Anywhere."

She looked at him in the oddest way. "Just walk? Land sakes, child, I've got things to do."

"But it's such a nice day, Mrs. Holly. Might rain tomorrow."

"Rain or shine, won't make a bit of difference to me." She sprayed something milky on the surface of the shelf, then wiped it off with her cloth.

"I don't mind the rain either," David said. Just the thought of rainy days on the mountain filled his mind with memories. "Daddy and I used to go out in the rain lots of times. There are some things you can't find any other time. Like the drops dancing on the leaves. And the rush of the rain when the wind gets behind it." David's lungs swelled. "Don't you just love to feel it, out in the open, where the wind gets a good chance to push?"

She turned to him sharply. "Honestly, David. I was saying I don't have time."

None of this made sense to David, not on such a beautiful day. "But do you have to keep all these things and clean, clean, clean them like this every day?"

"Well, I—"

"Couldn't you give them to somebody? Or maybe throw them away?"

Mrs. Holly picked up a crystal bird. "David, these things are valuable. They cost money and time and..." She turned back to her dusting. "Never mind, David. I should have known. Brought up the way you were...how could you appreciate fine things like these?"

David watched her toil. In a way she seemed so gloomy, like she could use some time to enjoy smelling some real flowers or maybe to watch an actual bird take flight. "I'm sorry, Mrs. Holly. It was only that I thought if you didn't have to clean so many things, you could maybe go walking more. Since you said you didn't have time."

Her eyes dropped down to the floor. Finally, she looked up again. "I know you meant all right, David. You run on, now. Go for a walk yourself. Let me get my chores done." She moved to that small oak desk, laden with cubbyholes.

After a moment's longing, David headed toward the door. How could he leave her there as down as she looked?

He turned back at the door as she pulled a stack of letters out. With what seemed like great affection, she untied the satin ribbon around them.

So that's what Mrs. Holly wanted to do. To have time to read her letters. Maybe they were from her son, John. Maybe reading them would lift her spirit. Just like Daddy's letter helped him.

As Mrs. Holly opened the first one, emotion washed over her face.

Quietly, David left the house. Daddy had a stack of letters like that, too. Back at their mountain cabin. Or maybe they'd been in that duffel bag Daddy left by the fallen log where they'd stopped. No matter how sick Daddy had gotten, those letters always made him feel better. Even better than that special tea Daddy taught him to make, from the moss on the north side of that certain grove of trees.

An idea struck as David headed down the road, toward the riverside woods. Maybe Mrs. Holly would feel better after a cup of that tea, too. If he could find Daddy's special moss there.

FOLLOWING HIS SILVER RIVER'S PATH through the forest comforted David. Daddy had still gone to the far country. But searching for that medicinal moss somehow bridged the broad expanse between them, connecting them all over again. Traipsing through those towering trees, drinking in the rush of water—it almost seemed like he'd found his way again, to their home on the mountain. And to the beautiful work Daddy said he should accomplish, at least for this day.

The symphony of it all rose from David's soul. Then, just as he lifted his violin to play what his surroundings inspired, he saw it. He gasped, nearly betraying his presence.

Ahead at the river's edge, a speckled fawn lapped a cool drink. Awe shimmered through David at the beauty of the creature. Frozen in place, he glanced around. The mother doe couldn't be far. Perhaps he could get a closer look if he stepped lightly enough.

Ever so carefully, David tiptoed through the fallen leaves and branches on the forest floor, holding his breath lest he scare the little deer.

With a sharp snap, a stick cracked below the ball of David's foot. Startled, the fawn looked up at him, then bounded into the brush.

Instantly, the cocking of a rifle split the silence, followed by a wild shot.

David whipped around, his heart furiously pounding. There crouched Eugene Streeter, training a rifle in the fawn's direction. His friends huddled beside him.

Again, Eugene fired. Another bullet whistled randomly into the brush. Eugene batted at a branch as he stood. "Dag! Never get the thing now."

Had the fawn escaped? David could only hope so. Daddy had showed him pictures and read to him about guns. After he'd heard shots fired in the foothills below the mountain. But never this loud or this close.

Another boy emerged from hiding and sneered at David. Like Eugene, he had on a bright orange vest. "My turn, now. You missed."

Eugene lowered the rifle. "Come on, Asa. I only missed because that weirdo there spooked it." He leveled a glare at David. "Thought I told you to stay outta my way." Eugene stooped to gather the rest of their kill. A rabbit and a squirrel hung limply from some sort of carrying device.

Bile churned in David's stomach. Aghast, he looked back and forth between the slain animals and Eugene. "What did you do that for?"

Eugene returned a sneer. "What's it to you, Freak Show?"

Horror assaulted David. "You were really trying to shoot that little fawn?"

"Duh." Asa snickered. "Kinda have to if you want to kill it."

"But why?" David braved another look at their dangling catch. Blood stained tawny fur. Flies buzzed about. "Is that what you did to that rabbit? You shot it?"

Eugene just shook his head at David. "You never had a lick of real fun in your life, did you?"

"Well, sure I did," David said. "But I never sent anything to the far country. Not on purpose."

"The far country?" Asa scratched his head as he turned to Eugene. "What's he talkin' about?"

"Who knows?" Eugene shrugged. "My dad said he's a loony-bin tramp." He whipped back around toward David. "Why don't you just git on outta here, Tramp. Tramp yourself off my property. 'Fore I set this here barrel on you."

David blanched. Whether or not Eugene meant to shoot him, too, David wouldn't stay to find out. Quickly, he turned and took off, back the same way he'd come, toward the road to the Hollys' farm.

Behind him, Eugene and Asa laughed. "Look at him go, Asa!" Eugene shouted at the top of his lungs. "Look at that crazy kid run!"

David didn't dare glance back. Hopefully, their cackling would alert that fawn, her mother, and every other forest creature to get as far as they could from Eugene Streeter's rifle.

DAVID PUT A PAPER NAPKIN into his lap. Napkins weren't something he and Daddy had used in the cabin. But Mr. Holly and Perry Larson put napkins in their laps and David reasoned that he should, too.

Mrs. Holly set a steaming bowl of corn chowder in front of each of them, beside a green salad. The aroma of her fresh-baked sourdough bread filled his nostrils.

Mr. Holly broke open a roll, without so much as a word of thanks. "Sounds like Streeter's boy, Eugene, all right."

Silently, David said his own grace, then blew on a spoonful of soup. "You think that was a real gun?"

"Don't shoot rabbits with no fake one," Perry Larson said.

"It's hunting season, David." Mrs. Holly pulled out a seat and joined them at the kitchen table. "You can't just go running anywhere in the woods."

Mr. Holly grunted. "Especially not them woods across the way. Streeter owns 'em. And I aim to stay on his good side."

"They're really his?" David could hardly believe it. How could one person own that beautiful forest? "Even the silver river that runs through there?"

With a swipe of his knife, Mr. Holly slathered butter across his bread. "That part to the right into town and all this land we're sittin' on, too. Leastways till I work the last of it off."

Mrs. Holly unfolded a paper napkin, too. "Eat your supper, now, David. Don't dawdle. We have an appointment to see our town's lawyer tonight. To figure out your...situation."

David set the spoonful of chowder into his mouth. It reminded him of the soup Daddy used to make from the vegetables in their garden. Creamy from the potatoes, with sweet kernels of corn laced with bits of caramelized onion.

"That corn is fresh from our field, you know." Mrs. Holly smiled at her husband as David took a second bite.

"Mighty right," Perry Larson added. "Those tomatoes, too. She grew those." He speared a forkful of salad. "Don't get no fresher than this here."

David would always miss Daddy's cooking, but something in the hearty goodness of this meal reassured him. If Mrs. Holly had anything to say about it, she'd make sure he didn't go hungry.

Barbara Holbrook sat at an elegantly arranged table as Tina Glaspell set dinner before her. Roasted baby red potatoes and French green beans garnished with slivered almonds complemented broiled salmon with a lemon-dill sauce. Barbara took in the scent. "You know, Tina, left to my own devises, I probably would have heated up the leftover stew from last night."

"I froze that for you to have over the weekend," Tina said. "When I'm not here."

She spread a linen napkin in her lap. "It smells wonderful. But you really don't need to go to so much trouble. Not on my account."

"No trouble, Ms. Holbrook—"

"Barbara. Remember?"

"Barbara, then. You're sure you don't want me to clean up?"

"No, it's fine."

Tina didn't look so sure.

"Really, Tina. It'll give me something to do after dinner. Other than rattle around this house by myself." Barbara gestured across the table. "Don't forget your check. It's there on the breakfront."

Tina collected the envelope and slid it into the pocket of her apron.

Barbara took a first bite. Heaven. Not a high-brow restaurant in the city could top Tina Glaspell's culinary skills.

Tina lingered. "I feel like I should thank you. For letting me keep my job, here. Your Aunt Grace, she was always good to me, too."

Barbara gazed around the expansive dining room. "She raised me here. She tell you that?"

A faint smile warmed Tina's face. "On average twice a day."

So like Aunt Grace. Affection mingled with grief as Barbara took in the echoing space. "I don't know. Maybe it's living here again, after my teensy little flat in the city. Or maybe it's just that she was here to fill it, but be honest. Does this place seem incredibly overblown to you?"

After a wistful look around, Tina bobbed her shoulders. "It's what people work for isn't it?"

Surrounded by everything a person could ever want, Barbara wasn't so sure.

Once Tina gathered her things and left, the void only increased. Not a sound but the creaking of the ancient timbers in the cooling evening air. Maybe she should sell the old place. Obligation choked back the thought, like an anchor's chain wrapped about her neck.

How could she even think of parting with everything that had made this place so grand over the ages? Eighteenth and nineteen-century antiques resonated across so many generations of Holbrook history. Some shipped all the way from England when her ancestors immigrated. Even if she could bring herself to part with the house and auction off all its contents, how could she let go of the land where her parents were buried?

Let alone Aunt Grace.

Now, a total stranger would occupy a space in their cemetery. Why had she been so quick to offer that plot? Not like a dead man would do a thing to keep her company. Barbara's eyes fell on Jack's manila envelope, resting on the breakfront. The paperwork he'd dutifully prepared. She searched her soul. Had Jack been the reason she'd offered their cemetery? Was this some subconscious way to court interaction with him?

Inside, Barbara kicked herself. What possessed her to even think that way? Obviously, Jack still had some connection to Charlotte. Why else would he have sat beside her at that meeting with so many other unoccupied chairs?

On the other hand, Jack had seemed skittish as a schoolboy delivering those papers earlier. Wearing a sport coat. And a tie, no less. With those brown, puppy-dog eyes of his. Like some long-repressed memory drew him back to her door. And he practically insisted upon returning to retrieve the paperwork personally. As if he didn't know she trusted him enough to sign it on the spot.

Barbara swallowed a last forkful, then glanced at her emptied plate. All those thoughts of Jack, and she'd downed her dinner, hardly tasting a morsel. She retrieved the linen napkin from her lap and dabbed her mouth, avoiding the Holbrook monogram. Even if her return had caught Jack's attention momentarily, the novelty would soon wear off.

Jack Gurnsey sat at his desk across from David and the Hollys, examining the boy's letters. The home office did double duty with his living room. But it had plenty of shelves for his law books and comfortable seating for his guests.

Not that Simeon Holly looked all that comfortable.

Ellen Holly's slender knitting needles clicked with each stitch, an infant cap forming. Certainly industrious. He'd give the woman that.

Simeon drummed his fingers on the armchair. "Ain't but so many babies being born, Woman."

Ellen just kept knitting.

Jack shook his head. Higgins called it right. Those letters David's father left behind didn't give him a thing to go on. Except to underscore the ten-year-old's naiveté when it came to anything to do with the contemporary world.

"You mind if I see that picture again, David?"

David pulled the tiny oval-framed picture out of his pocket and handed it to Jack.

He pored over the likeness. "Pretty, wasn't she?"

The boy's eyes took on a tender glow.

"And you don't know her name either?"

David shuffled toward the bookshelves. "Daddy always called her my angel-mother."

Jack looked up as his little sister peered in from the hall. Curiosity must have gotten the better of the girl, especially with this mysterious new boy in town. "Julia... Would you like to meet David?"

Julia's face reddened. "No, I was just... I have to feed Sally." She shot a look at David. "My rescue kitty." Without so much as a greeting to the Hollys, she rambled off toward the kitchen.

David may have bought the ruse, but Jack didn't. Julia had fed Sally just an hour ago.

He turned his attentions back toward David's letters. "Do you mind if I make a copy of these? That way you can keep your originals."

David nodded his approval. But his eyes bugged as Jack ran the letters through his photocopier. As if he'd never seen one before.

With a whir, duplicates slid out of the printer. "You can have both of these back now, David." He extended the letters to the boy. "I'm just hoping they might help us figure things out somehow."

David's jaw slacked as he surveyed the many volumes on Jack's shelves. "Have you read all these books?"

"Most of them," Jack replied. "When I was in law school."

"Is that your work? Being a lawyer?" David traced his fingers across a matched set of volumes.

Inadequacy washed over Jack. The same wave that doused him every time anyone questioned what he did for a living. Facts were facts. Odd legal jobs seemed more of an avocation, now that he'd left his practice in the city. With the market so flooded, even that had dwindled. These days, full-time nanny described his occupation better.

Jack exchanged a glance with Simeon, who averted what seemed a disapproving gaze. Ellen pulled another length from her skein and kept on knitting.

The boy's question still hung in the air, challenging every shred of self-worth Jack had left. "Yes, David. That's my work. Anyway, I should say it used to be."

David sat on the Hollys' front steps. In the spill of moonlight, he read Daddy's letters to himself. Again. Soon, he would have those words memorized, hidden in his heart. Where he could listen to what Daddy said no matter what. And no one could reach in and take those words away.

Mrs. Holly tied off a knitted baby cap and snipped the yarn with her scissors. "There we go."

David looked the cap over. "Who is that for?"

"Oh, I don't know," she said. "Maybe Esther Mullins' baby, maybe Charlie and Sarah Pepper's. Between Grace Holbrook and me, I suppose we knitted for half the babies in the county. Sure do miss my friend, Grace. She's the one that got me started, you know. Rich as she was, could've bought out every cap in *Sears-Roebuck*. But...I guess there's still something about doing it yourself. Anyway, that's what Grace always said."

David nodded. "Daddy used to say the same thing. When you make something yourself, you don't just make an object. You make a memory. You give a bit of your life to the person that gift is for."

"I don't so much understand it all, David. But I do know something of what your daddy talked about in that letter."

"You do?" He drew his knees up to his chest.

She rotated the baby cap on her fingertips. "I know it's next to nothing. Nothing fancy. Nothing worth nothing. But our itty-bitty hospital don't have much. And it's something I can do to make being born just a little nicer."

David warmed inside. "That's the work you do. To make the world more beautiful."

"I guess." She set the little cap aside and began to wind the excess yarn around its ball. "Fact is, except for going to the market and church, I almost never leave this farm." Mrs. Holly scanned the property. "That's no complaint. I like it here. But I got to feeling like doing something outside myself awhile ago. And this is what I can do."

David gazed dreamily at the night sky. "Daddy said there's a beautiful work for me out there, too. I just wish I knew what it was."

She tucked her knitting back into a calico bag. "You're just a boy, David. You got time."

"Not once it's gone," he said. "That's what Daddy always told me. A minute ticks by. An hour passes. And I should always try to fill it, the best way I can. Don't you think that's right, Mrs. Holly?"

She set her eyes on the letters in his hands. "Shame we didn't get to know that Daddy of yours."

Warmth spread through David. "You would have loved Daddy. Like I do."

"Yes." Mrs. Holly rose to her feet and picked up her knitting bag. "It seems so." Silently, she stood there a moment. Then, with a shake of her head, she headed back inside. "Come on in soon, David. High time to call it a night."

"I will." David leaned back against the post supporting the porch. Once more, he read through his letter, the one Daddy wrote especially for him. A hole opened up in David's heart. The divide between where he sat and the distant far country sprawled endlessly between them. Why did Daddy have to go so soon?

David's eyes filled. How he missed the life they'd had. Daddy's smile. The astonishing melodies that rang out whenever Daddy played his violin. The wisdom in most everything he ever had to say.

How he could venture on without Daddy, David couldn't imagine. But Daddy had said that he should, so somehow, he'd set his mind to it. He would find that hope Daddy said awaited him, out there in the world. That beautiful work Daddy said he should do. Exactly what that work was, David didn't know. But whatever life brought, with everything in him, David would set it all to music.

10

Barbara sat on her bed, staring at Jack's manila envelope. Telling, the way she managed to avoid opening the thing for so long. Like something inside would jump out and bite her. She chided herself. All she'd find enclosed would be a legal document. Knowing Jack, she could sign it sight unseen.

She kicked off her shoes and scrunched back into the collection of pillows against her headboard. The envelope hadn't even been sealed. Nothing as personal as Jack having moistened the flap. Just that flimsy metal clasp to secure it.

Time to get this over with. Barbara opened the envelope and pulled out the contents. A hand-labeled note slipped to the floor. What? She got up to retrieve it, then settled back onto the bed. This one, Jack had sealed. He'd written her name across the envelope. Not Ms. Holbrook as he'd referred to her before. Barbara.

Jack's scrawl had matured, but it echoed across the decades with fond memories. Notes furtively passed in grade school. Fanning that long ago flame she'd held for him, only to have it soundly snuffed out in the city.

"Okay," she murmured, though no one could hear. "Let's do this." She shoved her thumb under the flap, tore the little envelope open, and extracted the handwritten card.

> *This is all fairly boilerplate, but feel free to let me know if you'd like any changes.*
>
> *—Jack*

Boilerplate indeed. That's all the note could claim to be either. One standard lawyer-to-client sentence. Nothing at all individual. Other than the fact that he'd used their first names. Why had Jack even bothered? And what power did he hold over her that she'd leapt into hope that way, tantalized to see if he'd written something more?

Barbara flipped the card over. As if she'd find anything else there. She set the note aside and picked up the document. That addendum to the deed she'd inherited. Everything that had come between them.

If only her parents hadn't left the money for boarding school in trust. Aunt Grace would have kept her in public school with Jack all those years. No doubt, her parents had arranged to send her away for private high schooling with the very best of intentions. In its own way, Wellingham Heights Academy had been good for her, helping her focus on academics and social graces. Upwardly mobile young men.

Instead of creek-fording, tree-climbing boys.

Boarding school prepared her to enter society—white-gloved debutante ball and all. Fair enough, graduating from Wellingham poised her for an Ivy League education. No question about that. But what a monumental let-down it had been, after all that hoopla blew over and the cold shoulder of reality turned so haughtily against her. Literally hundreds of applications, all without a solitary opportunity. Apparently, this world had no interest in anything she had to offer.

Jack Gurnsey included.

Simeon Holly watched his wife turn down John's bed for David. Sure didn't take no pop TV shrink to tell where that woman's mind had headed. Like wild grass, that boy had sprung up overnight, wrapping himself clear around Ellen's heart. "Don't know why you bother. Boy sleeps on the hard floor."

Ellen smoothed the top of the sheet over the edge of the comforter. "Well, maybe turning it down will make it more inviting this time."

Much as he hated to, might as well bring things out in the open. Ellen would never say a thing if he didn't. Wasn't her way. No, she'd just brood about it in silence, expecting him to figure things out. "I suppose with that fiddle playin' and all, he's reminding you of John."

A sad arc curved on Ellen's lips. "Been a long time since there was a boy in this house."

Simeon checked around. The door to the hall bath remained closed. Still, he lowered his voice, lest David overhear. "All the same, you shouldn't get too attached. They already called the county office about findin' family."

She turned to John's dresser and tugged a drawer open. "David's got nobody."

"We don't know that, Ellen." He paced around to her right. "This here's the twenty-first century. Can't just keep a stray boy this day and age. Not like Julia Gurnsey kept that cat. Got to go through channels with kids."

"I know." Ellen pulled out a pair of John's pajamas.

"Who knows who might be lookin' for the boy." Simeon followed her back toward the bed. "That vagrant fella could've snatched David away to that mountain. Brainwashed him somehow. Filled his head with all manner of malarkey. Might not have been his real daddy at all. You think o' that?"

"Now, who's talking crazy?" She laid the pajamas out neat as a pin. Like that boy would pay her tidiness a second of mind.

"Come on, Ellen. Use the head God give ya. David might be on some milk carton. Or missin' children's list, for all we know. There's a reason that man never told the kid his last name. And say what you will, I can't think of a good one."

She slid a perturbed gaze toward him, clearly not believing a word.

Simeon expelled some air. "Not like we can afford to keep him anyhow. Not with our note comin' due."

"Nonsense." At the creak of the bathroom door, Ellen hushed her tone. "Your crop out there'll more than cover our note with Streeter. Besides, the little bit David eats is hardly going to break us."

"All the same," he said. "You're best watchin' yourself. No point gettin' your heart broke twice."

David appeared at the door.

Simeon turned. "You wash up good?"

The boy extended his hands for inspection. "Yes, Sir."

He patted the top of John's comforter. "You'll sleep up here in the bed tonight, David. You'll like it. Besides, I don't want nobody down the pike stirrin' up trouble, sayin' I made you sleep on no hard wood floor."

Ellen put a motherly hand on David's shoulder. "Say your prayers. You know how to do that, don't you, David?"

"Daddy taught me," David replied. "He said it's kind of like the way I breathe. So, anytime, I can just blow anything that's inside me out, then fill up with what comes back to me. Is that how you do it, Mrs. Holly?"

"Well..." She floundered a bit, then shot Simeon a flustered look. "Something like that, I suppose. Night, then."

With a hand to her back, Simeon led his wife to the door. He didn't have much call these days for lovey-dovey displays of affection. Especially not in front of other people. But as soon as he stroked her, she followed him out and closed the door behind them.

Thank goodness that still worked.

Jack switched off his living room lamps for the night. Something about the stillness soothed him. By now, Julia would be slumbering. Better be. If she stopped texting her friends at the electronics curfew he'd set. A pang of envy tweaked him. At least she had friends to chat up.

He drew aside the sheers covering the front bay window. Across the street, beyond the tree-lined stream, the lights from Sunnycrest dimmed. Barbara must be retiring for the night, too.

Julia descended the stairs, cradling that kitten of hers. Sally.

"I thought you were in bed."

She shuffled his way. "I thought you were surfing around for stuff on that boy."

Jack's eyes remained fixed on the turret of Sunnycrest. "Came up blank."

Julia wandered closer. "Whatcha looking at?"

Caught, he shifted his gaze down the street. He pointed to a slumped man, stumbling down the block. "Luke Dowd, drinking up most of what he made today. Digging that grave."

"Whose grave? The homeless man?"

His chest deflated. "David's father. Alive when I saw him. Gone now. I don't know why I didn't take more of an interest. I could have asked his name. Should have. Shame, how opportunity slips by."

"Eugene Streeter said that kid's wacko. Asa thinks so, too."

Reluctantly, Jack let the sheers drop and turned to his sister. "Since when do you listen to Eugene Streeter?"

"I don't. He was just all blah-dee, blah, blah about David on this website I go to," she said. "Before nine p.m., that is. When I totally shut everything off, exactly like you told me I have to." Her lips crinkled.

"Yeah, right." Sally the kitten purred as Jack scratched behind her ears. "Not easy losing a father."

"I know," Julia said. "I get it."

Jack nodded. "I mean, who knows how long David will be around here, but... Maybe you can make up your own mind about him."

"I guess." Julia turned and headed up the stairs, skipping those purple fuzzy slippers over every other step. "Goodnight again."

"Good night. Sleep tight. And don't let the snuggle bunnies bite."

Julia paused to lean over the rail. "Have I mentioned lately how completely lame that saying is for anyone over age six?"

Jack chuckled. "I'll make a note."

"Anyway, you can still use it," Julia said. "Since Mom and Dad did." She straightened to resume her climb. "But I'm just saying..."

"Right." Jack rubbed at his jaw. Julia seemed so much worldlier than he'd felt at her age. Back when he'd imagined himself some kind of medieval prince, fording the moat to Sunnycrest. Then scaling the sycamore, all for a chance to steal a few moments with Barbara. Even then, she'd been the prettiest girl he'd ever seen. Like a princess, trapped in that tower across the way.

But times had certainly changed.

And not so very much for the better.

David looked across the room at the too-tall bed. There would be no avoiding it this time. Not after what Mr. Holly said. Maybe he'd get used to it. Might as well put on those pajamas and climb up those little wooden steps. Give that Goliath of a bed a try.

As David pulled his jacket off, the gold he'd been hiding slipped out of his pockets and jangled to the floor. David's heart caught in his throat. Had Mr. and Mrs. Holly heard that? What if they found out about the gold and thought he'd stolen it? Like that woman, Ada Grundle. The one who branded him a thief.

Quickly dropping to his knees, David gathered the coins. Keeping them in his pockets might not be the best idea. Especially as warm as he got chopping wood for Mr. Holly. No, he had to take that jacket off and set it aside. Mrs. Holly had already asked to wash the rest of his clothes. So, what if she tried to clean the jacket and discovered the gold inside?

David scanned the room carefully. Daddy said to hide the gold, and there had to be a good place to do that. Somewhere Mrs. Holly wouldn't clean. Or maybe not so very often as she appeared to clean most everything else.

He wandered toward the many books on John Holly's shelves. The edge just in front of the books had been wiped, but the thin trail of dust lining the very base of each book told him something. Looked like she hadn't pulled the books out of place for a long time.

Ever so stealthily, David removed a dictionary and tucked his sack of gold behind it. He slid the volume back into place where the dust-line marked its position. Now he could rest easily, with Daddy's treasure secure.

Once David scaled it, the too-tall bed turned out much better than he'd imagined. With those downy feather pillows under his head and that fluffy comforter nestled over him, it beckoned him into the arms of sleep. Kind of like climbing into one of his cloud-boats in the sky. Sailing away on a dream.

And music.

What was that music?

David scanned an expansive theater. A hundred or more instruments stretched across a dazzling stage, being tuned to an oboe's perfect pitch. The warm-up of a symphony orchestra.

Suddenly much younger, David followed a beautiful young woman down the aisle. Mama. Not many four-year-olds gained entry to this ornate concert hall, but Mama still said he could come. Another pretty woman trailed just behind them, her hand on his small shoulder.

"Excuse us," the woman said to an elegantly dressed couple they passed. The lady's dress sparkled as she pulled her skirt aside to swish by them.

His mother stopped, her gown the color of a blushing rose. "Here we are, Honey. This row. I'll go in first. Then you can sit right between us. But we have to be quiet, now. Daddy is about to start."

The younger woman followed them in and took the seat to his left. She guided his eyes back toward the front. "Look, David. There he is."

Lights illuminated the stage. Applause thundered as a virtuoso violinist stepped forward, dressed in a crisply pressed tuxedo.

Daddy.

Awestruck, little David watched his father as he acknowledged the orchestra behind him, then set his bow to begin.

Mama wrapped an affectionate arm around David and smiled. Her eyes gleaming with loving admiration, she turned back to the stage.

David woke with a start. Just as quickly as he'd opened his eyes he shut them tight again.

If only he could return to that dream, that wonderful place and time. When his angel-mother sat close beside him. When Daddy's strings reverberated with such passion, and the whole hall sat rapt at his brilliance.

11

Dawn's golden glow peered over the horizon. Still wearing pajamas, David tracked with Mr. Holly's farmhand. "There was a full orchestra. Over a hundred pieces. Just like Daddy always talked about. And my angel-mother, she was there, too."

Perry Larson prepped Mr. Holly's truck, never missing a beat. "Did she have her some wings on?"

"No, angel-mothers don't have wings," David replied. "They're not really angels. They just live with the angels. In the far country."

"Oh." The farmhand chuckled. "Well then, I s'pose I stand corrected."

Mr. Holly strode toward them. "Boy!"

David whipped around. "I'm going to start chopping soon, Mr. Holly. I just had to tell Perry Larson what I dreamed."

"Dreamin's for nighttime, Boy. Don't you know that?" Mr. Holly gestured toward his field. "Perry's got plenty to do this mornin' without gettin' his ear bent. You and me—we got to clean up, David. Go to town. Woman's comin' here from county Social Services to talk to you." Mr. Holly pointed him toward the house. "Run upstairs now, to Mrs. Holly. She'll help you find somethin' respectable to wear."

David found Mrs. Holly in the room where he'd slept, selecting a cotton shirt from that storage box in her son's closet. "This should fit. I'll just need to press it up nice for you."

Just as he'd suspected, David's regular clothes sat atop Mrs. Holly's laundry basket. Including his jacket. Good thing he'd hidden those coins. David's gaze wandered to a black violin case where it rested on the closet's top shelf. Not like his or Daddy's, but a familiar shape all the same. "Is that your son's violin?"

Mrs. Holly shook out the shirt. "He played a while. Nothing like you, but... John went on to other pursuits. His art mostly. But I just never could part with the thing. I got these clothes down from the attic just last month. I was going to send them on to John, seeing as he has a boy of his own, now. But styles have changed, and we don't so much..."

Wistfully, she trailed off. Then, as if to shoo a troubling notion away, she held the shirt up to David. "Anyway, I like the way this'll look on you."

Not twenty minutes later, the three of them piled into the cab of Mr. Holly's pick-up truck. Rumbling down the road to town between them brought that dream back to David's mind. Even in his sleep, how wonderful it had been to hear Daddy play, nestled between Mama and that pretty young woman.

David searched his mind. With that blonde hair of hers, that woman seemed vaguely familiar, like he'd seen her before. But just as the connection seemed so close, it disintegrated, escaping his grasp. Had that been just a dream or had Mama really taken him to hear Daddy play with the symphony, when he'd only been four-years-old?

Mr. Holly nudged David, breaking his reverie. "See now...this here's Hinsdale. For what it's worth."

The town's quaintly lettered sign announced the year of its foundation. A train idled at the station to their right. Captivated, David pointed past Mrs. Holly. "That's the train! Daddy said we'd take the train to get to the world."

"Settle down, Boy." Mr. Holly pulled to a stop at a corner sign. "Now, don't you go talking goofy to that woman from county. Nothin' about playin' that fiddle for no flower people or dreamin' about no Orchestra o' Life. Or sailin' off on some kinda cloud-boat to some far country, ya hear?"

Still, David enthralled at the sights. Store after store lined the street on the way into town. Houses stretched around a manicured park with picnic benches and a gazebo, their white picket fences framing the town square. And people. Men, women, and children milled around. Some hustling along the sidewalk, in and out of businesses, and some playing with dogs in the grass.

"This is town?" David asked.

Mr. Holly pointed to a three-story house ahead. "That's Streeter's Bed and Breakfast, there." An enormous flowering tree dominated the front yard. Never had David seen such an astounding canopy. "Oh, can't we stop? That's the most beautiful tree!"

Mrs. Holly patted his arm. "Later, David. You do a good job in there...and maybe we can come back."

Simeon glowered. That social worker from county sure had herself a bad case of the sniffles. The woman had barely introduced herself before she'd had to blow her nose. And wouldn't it be just a fine whoop-de-doo if they all came down with whatever mess this woman had.

Ellen fished a tissue from her purse and passed it to the social worker. "Would this help, Miss Boles?"

"Thank you." Miss Boles tossed her used hankie into the trash and accepted the fresh one readily. "I should have thought to bring more, coming out here to the country."

For a while they just sat there while Miss Boles pored over all the papers in her file. Like the clue to some deep, dark mystery would come jumping out to grab her any second. Not likely. Simeon couldn't imagine she'd find any more than they had. Next to nothing, far as he could tell.

"Well, then," Miss Boles said. "We seem to have a few blanks here, but I can still start working on placement." Again, she wiped her reddened nose.

Simeon covered his mouth.

"Not to worry," Miss Boles said. "I'm not contagious. It's just the pollen this time of year. Can't take all this fresh air." Suddenly, her whole body jerked with a sneeze. "*Excusez-moi!*"

David leaned over toward her. "*A vos souhaits, Mademoiselle.*"

Simeon felt his jaw drop. And Ellen, she looked just as stunned.

Right away, Miss Boles launched into some loco exchange with David. "*Dis-moi, David, parles-tu francais?*"

David's eyes lit like a Christmas tree. "*Oui, oui, Mademoiselle. Mon pere m'a enseigne de parler la langue, et je l'adore.*"

Hard to tell what grew quicker—Ellen's shock or that itch in Simeon's craw. They'd best be done with this nonsense, just as soon as possible.

Still, the social worker went on, as if normal English-speaking folks weren't even sitting there. "*Moi, je l'ai etudiee pendant toutes les annees scholaires. J'ai toujours pense que c'etait la plus belle langue.*"

Excitedly, David replied. "*Mon pere et moi, nous avons passe des jours ensembles parlant tout en francais. C'est de cette facon que j'ai appris la langue. Nous avons discute toutes les choses sur la montagne, dans le ciel—*"

Abruptly, Simeon raised his hands. "Now, hold on here. I'm a busy man. I ain't got all day for jawwin' away in no kind o' foreign gibber-jabber."

Miss Boles sat back. She turned a penitent gaze on him. "You'll have to forgive me, Mr. Holly. It's just so rare to meet someone—a child at that—who is so fluent in French. Tell me, David, do you speak any other languages?"

"No, not really," David sat back. "There's Latin, but nobody speaks that anymore. And I only really read Italian. So much music is sung in Italian, you know."

The social worker made a note. "And I also understand you're quite accomplished on the violin."

David ran a hand along his case. "I'm not as good as my father was."

Again, she scribbled something into her file. "Well, maybe, if you work hard, you can get into a good music school someday. There are exceptional schools out there, conservatories with fine teachers who can challenge you to cultivate your gifts. Do you think you'd like that, David?"

David's face practically shone.

Simeon glanced at his watch. Half the morning had slipped right through their fingers. "Any chance we can get to the here and now?"

"Yes, of course," Miss Boles said. "Placement. It can take longer with an older child. Ah..." She set a finger below her nostrils. "Pardon me..." Once more, she sneezed.

Timid as a mouse, Ellen raised her hand. "I was just wondering. About what the possibilities were, uh...as far as the foster situation goes."

Simeon poked her with his elbow. "Not in front of the boy, Ellen."

The social worker turned to David. "It looks like Mr. and Mrs. Holly and I have a few more things to go over. Would you like to wait for us just outside, David?"

David didn't take any convincing. He just grabbed that fiddle case of his and took off.

"Don't get far," Ellen called after him.

"I won't," David replied as he slipped through the door.

Every confounded day, Ellen kept acting more and more attached to that kid. And all Simeon could do was thank heaven above that David would soon be gone. He'd be placed within the foster care system, with folks much younger than they. The sooner county did that, the better. Best to get David settled somewhere else. Far out of sight.

Before the boy sunk his roots another inch deeper into Ellen's heart.

Sheltered from view behind the velvet drapes of her library, Barbara watched the activity outside in Sunnycrest's family cemetery.

Jack and Luke helped Cyrus Higgins and Buck Taylor carry the vagrant's casket to its resting place.

Death didn't discriminate between rich or poor. Almost poetic to think of this homeless man, lying side-by-side with those of so-called loftier station. Barbara's parents might not have approved of those papers she held in her hands, but Aunt Grace would have backed the decision one hundred percent. Aunt Grace always saw this life in the bigger picture, through the lens of eternity. Barely a moment and our time on earth would be gone, she'd say.

Tina rapped on the doorjamb, cleaning supplies in tow. "You mind if I dust in here?"

"Not at all, Tina. Go ahead."

Barbara glanced at the signed paperwork, then focused on Jack, outside in the distance. He hadn't come to her door for the papers.

Not yet, anyway.

Could this be his way of drawing her out there, compelling her to come to him? Of course, he'd approached her last. The ball sat squarely in her court. Still, how could it be right to sully such a solemn occasion with their on-going awkwardness?

Enough second guessing. Barbara extended the papers toward her housekeeper. "Actually, Tina... Could you take these out to Mr. Gurnsey for me? It'll save him the trip to the house."

Tina set her bucket down and accepted the papers. "Glad to do it." Tina glanced out the window at the small gathering of men. "But are you sure?"

An affectionate smile crossed Barbara's face. Somehow, Tina knew. "I suppose my aunt told you."

"Not directly," Tina said. "But I've seen plenty of pictures in the scrapbooks she made, back when you two were growing up. Toward the end, she liked to go through those photos with me. So, I couldn't help notice you were friends."

Barbara watched Jack outside. Ironic that even now he seemed so far away. "Sometimes I think that was somebody else."

Tina laced her fingers together. "Still appears to have an eye for you."

All Barbara could do was shake her head. Maybe at one time, Jack had. "When we were kids we had these little signals, you know? I'd stand up there...in the window of the turret like some—I don't know—quasi princess or whatever. I'd wave once for 'I'm coming over.' Or two waves with a gap in between meant 'you come over here.' No guessing. Never had to say a thing, just..." Barbara waved a nostalgic hand. "Cheesy, huh?"

"Sounds pretty sweet to me," Tina said.

"Yeah. Maybe it was, but then..." The memory darkened in her mind. "Leaving the city, his practice, so soon after I'd settled there. Jack seeing someone else... Those were his choices." Once again, she mulled over the decision before her. But in reality, nothing had changed. "I didn't come back to Hinsdale for Jack Gurnsey. And it's best I don't send that message."

Though Tina didn't seem to grasp Barbara's logic, she accepted the envelope of papers and left without another word.

Barbara watched Tina hurry across the stone pavers through the rose garden, heading toward the family cemetery. Tina probably meant well, but what did she really know? After all, Tina had suggested Luke for the grave-digging job. Somewhere under Luke's scruffy look hid the potential for a ruggedly attractive guy. But the alcohol on the man's breath—that hadn't done a thing to bolster Barbara's confidence in Tina's judgment about men.

The closer Tina got to the gravesite, the tighter the knot in her stomach got. More and more, that's how things rolled with her when it came to Luke. Why she still cared enough to help get him this job, she couldn't figure. Unless somehow hard work could turn him around, into the man she'd first thought he could be.

Time and time again, she'd been on her knees about the guy. Now and then, she'd get her hopes up. When he repeatedly swore off the booze. But alcohol had its hooks deep into Luke. Just like her parents, though they'd never cop to it.

Why had she taken up with Luke, even knowing how the bottle could drown a person? Grace Holbrook—she'd voiced her concerns about Luke, too.

How a woman as alive as Grace could just be gone made no sense to Tina at all. Sure was nicer to think of her resting in God's arms than under the sod of that cemetery.

Tina slowed as she neared the grave. Jack Gurnsey and Cyrus Higgins held some ropes on one side, easing the plain pine box into that freshly dug hole. Luke and Buck Taylor stood at the opposite edge, their forearms taut with exertion. Once they lowered the coffin into place, Luke jumped into the hole to salvage the ropes from underneath. In fairness, it seemed he'd taken the job seriously. He hadn't embarrassed her for suggesting him in the first place.

Tina extended the envelope of papers to Jack. "Looks like you're good to go on this. Far as the owner is concerned."

Jack craned his head over Tina's shoulder. "Is anybody coming out for this?"

Not hard to read the man's meaning. "No." Tina looked back at the house. Just in time to see Barbara drop the curtain and step back from the library window. "Not far as I know."

Jack's face fell. He must have seen that, too.

"It's just us," Higgins added, totally missing Jack's intent. "Simeon Holly didn't want to tell the boy. Wouldn't understand anyhow."

Jack turned back to Tina and accepted the envelope. "Thank you, then."

Luke and Buck grabbed a pair of shovels, propped against a tree.

Tina balked. Were they seriously going to throw dirt in that hole, without even a stitch of ceremony? She shot Luke a glassy stare. "Isn't somebody gonna say somethin'?"

Higgins shrugged sheepishly. "We didn't call for the preacher. Nobody actually knew the man."

Tina splayed her hands out. "He was a livin', breathin' person, wasn't he? He was somebody's daddy. I like to think that makes you worth some kind of somethin'."

Luke leaned on his shovel. "Look, Baby, I got places to be. I'm gettin' on with this."

Tina pointed at Luke demandingly. "You can wait two seconds, Luke Dowd." But as she scanned the men's faces, one thing became clear. Not a one of them had any plan to step up. Not Higgins, not Buck, or even Jack.

And certainly not Luke.

She blew out an exasperated puff. "I'll say it."

Luke rolled his eyes and leaned back against a tree trunk. Buck stopped, too. Only Jack and Higgins had the decency of lowering their heads.

Now, what to do?

Not like she'd turned into some expert on how to pay proper respects. But no time like the present to figure it out.

Tina marched to a nearby rhododendron. She snapped off a blossom, then returned to the rim of the grave. She narrowed her gaze across the hole. "Bow your head. Do it, Luke."

Still propped against that tree, he crossed one leg over the other. "Look at the never-married mother of two findin' Jesus."

"Better him than you." Tina bit her lip, resisting the urge to say more.

Buck elbowed Luke. "Mouthy, ain't she?"

Luke rolled his eyes. "Ain't they all?"

Suddenly, Jack stood at Tina's side. "You might want to consider who got you this job, Luke. And the fact that we're still holding your pay."

Begrudgingly, Luke lowered his head. Though he never closed his eyes. Not that Tina saw anyway. Clear enough, he wouldn't go along with this, even to humor her. But she could give this burial a touch of human dignity.

Tina raised her eyes toward the sky. What had she heard them say over Grace Holbrook, not so long ago? She drew in some air, then emptied her lungs. "Okay. So Lord, here lies..." She completely blanked. No way out of this one but to stop and ask somebody. "What was his kid's name, again?"

"David," Higgins replied in concert with Jack.

Anew, Tina turned to the heavens. "Here lies David's daddy. None of us, we didn't know him. But I figure you did, so... I guess, please just...take him on home. Amen."

Tina stooped over the head of the grave, close as she could reach toward the wooden box at the bottom. She dropped the flowers in there first, then straightened up, brushed off her knees, and gave a wave to Luke. "Okay. Go on."

She'd pay for taking that tone with him later, no doubt. But Tina didn't care. Sometimes you did what seemed right to do, no matter the trouble it caused.

12

David peered out the double wooden doors of Hinsdale's Town Hall. What a wonderland of tantalizing sights around the square. So many cars. Bicycles, too. David stepped back as, in a blur, Eugene, Asa, and another boy darted by on foot. Once they'd passed, David descended the granite steps and set off down the sidewalk ringing the square.

Just past the businesses, David came upon a small white house. Though the garden tangled with wild overgrowth, an enormous red peony burst through the brambles. He unhitched the gate to get a closer look. Ah, what a melody rose from within at the sight. Quickly, he opened his case and raised his violin.

"Ahem." A brunette woman stood at the gate, a bag of groceries in her arms. She would have been much lovelier except for that scowl on her face.

"What on earth do you think you're doing in my front yard?"

David looked up. "I'm looking for my work, Ma'am. I'm David."

She eyed him suspiciously. "I'll thank you not to call me Ma'am. I'm Miss Somers to my students. And you may as well know that times are tight. I have no intent spending what little they give me to teach here, paying you to weed."

"Oh, I wasn't asking to garden." David turned back to the blossom. "It's this peony. It's as pretty as they come already. Don't you love the way it's bursting out through all this mess?"

She raised a single brow. "This mess, you say?"

"Some things, well..." David gazed around. "They're just so full of life that nothing at all can choke them out."

What hint of pleasantry had been in Miss Somers' voice soured. "You're that homeless boy, aren't you?"

David shook his head. "I have a home, up on the mountain. Just not here in town."

She switched her bag to her left arm, probably so she could wag her index finger. "Well, lesson number one about getting along in civilization: don't come through someone's gate uninvited. It's called trespassing."

"Trespassing?"

"That's right. And they shoot trespassers in some counties."

David's eyes widened. After being on the wrong end of Eugene Streeter's rifle, that didn't sound so inviting.

"Go on, now," Miss Somers said. "Shoo! Before I call Sheriff Wahl on you." She kept sweeping him away with the back of her hand till he grabbed his violin case and left the yard. Then, she locked the gate behind him, bustled up her steps, and disappeared into her house.

It didn't seem that she'd really call the sheriff. But all the same, David hurried away, down the sidewalk. No point in taking any chances. Especially since there were so many other things to see. And no telling how much longer Mr. and Mrs. Holly would stay inside with that social worker.

There, just a couple of doors down, David drank in the sight that magnificent flowering tree, in front of Mr. Streeter's Bed & Breakfast. Its canopy stretched out like an umbrella, shading most of the yard. Butterflies fluttered from bloom to bloom. "Well, you are a sight, aren't you? How could I even start to play..."

The roar of a chainsaw broke David's reverie. A man dressed in protective gear headed toward the tree. Just then, Mr. Streeter stepped out to his porch and clapped his stout hands. "Get a move on, Charlie. Ain't got all day."

David whipped between Mr. Streeter and that noisy chain saw, agape at what seemed to be Mr. Streeter's plan. It couldn't be. Yet it was. Horrified, David screamed. "Nooooo!"

"Get going, there, Pepper! Remember who's payin' you."

Mr. Charlie Pepper trained the chainsaw on the massive tree trunk.

David dove at him in desperation. "You can't!"

Still Mr. Pepper throttled his engine. "Hold on, there, Kiddie. This is dangerous equipment."

"But you can't hurt this tree!" David threw himself against the trunk.

"Oh, for pity's sake." Streeter lumbered down his steps and into the fray.

Townsfolk slowed to watch. David scanned their faces. Most, he didn't recognize. But there was Mrs. Mollie Tate, who fed him breakfast the day the letter from Daddy came. That lawyer, Jack Gurney's little sister, Julia, sidled over to Mrs. Tate.

Mrs. Tate nodded toward David. "Got us a regular tree hugger."

Julia traded a grin with her. "Streeter's gonna pop a gut."

Streeter blustered his way to David. "Now, you wait yourself a minute here, Boy. This is my yard and my tree, and I'll have it cut if I want." He whirled back to Mr. Charlie Pepper. "Charlie, let her rip."

"No!" David cried. "Don't, Mr. Pepper. Please!"

Mrs. Tate cupped her hand by her mouth. "Thing's pretty, Streeter. I say you leave it."

"Go on!" Streeter waved a demanding hand toward Mr. Pepper. "I hired you to cut down the tree, Pepper. So, cut the tree!"

A reluctant look on his face, Mr. Pepper revved his chainsaw's engine again.

"You're not doing it! You're not!" David lunged in front of Mr. Pepper, spreading his arms wide. "How could you kill something so beautiful? Something that waited through the cold all winter, just to sing out with all of these flowers and leaves, all about the One who grew it?"

Mr. Pepper bit at his lip, then he shut his motor off again and looked at Streeter.

"I'm warnin' you, Charlie..." Streeter narrowed his gaze.

"What am I s'posed to do, Streeter?" Mr. Pepper took off his protective goggles. "He's just a kid. I got one o' my own on the way."

Mr. Streeter steamed. "Which is why you should think o' who's payin' ya. You want the job or not?"

Mr. Pepper looked past David to the gathering crowd. Even Miss Somers had come back out. He spun back to his employer. "Sometimes, you know, Streeter... It just ain't worth it."

With that, Mr. Pepper took his chainsaw and left, prompting a smattering of applause from the crowd.

Julia whistled through her teeth as Mrs. Tate blew a kiss to the tree.

With an angry glare at David, Mr. Streeter stormed back up to his house. He flung the door open, went inside, then slammed it with a thud.

Simeon Holly's blood boiled. "Blast it, woman! We can't take that boy in."

Ellen just kept up her infernal knitting. "But Simeon..."

"But nothin'!"

"How many ways I got to say it, Ellen? We got to keep peace with Streeter here. You think that man's gonna cut me one ounce o' slack on my note, now?"

Ellen glanced out to where David sat on the porch steps. She reached up to close the window. "He didn't know."

"He don' know nothin'!" Simeon said. "All this talk bout goin' into the world, findin' his work. Face it, the boy ain't got the sense God give a turnip."

With a maddening calm, Ellen stretched out another length of yarn. "He's been educated."

"I'm talkin' horse sense, Ellen. He ain't got a bit o' what it takes to get along, much less work."

She raised watering eyes from her needles. "He's got more than you think, Simeon."

Simeon paced away a step, then turned back. "He's got your heart, that's what he's got. You give it to him, even after I told you not to."

Ellen didn't deny it. She just kept right on with her knitting and purling. "I can't help what I feel."

"Yes, you can," he replied. "You can yank your head down from them cloud-boats he's got ya in and look at what's real." He threw his hands up. Why couldn't she get this? "We ain't livin' in no dream land. I got bills to pay, Ellen. An' hard dirt to farm on real land we don't own yet."

She gave him a pitiful glance. "He means good."

He leveled as serious a look as he could at her. "This is the last time I'll say it, Ellen. There's no place here for a boy like that, no place in this world."

At that, Ellen stopped. She stared at him full in the face. "Like there was no place for John?"

Simeon winced. It wasn't often she touched on that tender old wound. But it wouldn't do a bit of good to let on how it smarted. "All John's fiddle playin', it never amounted to squat."

Ellen just shook her head. "It wasn't fiddling that took John away from us. It was his art, and you two never seeing eye to eye." Finally, she looked up, tears streaking. "It's not that there wasn't a place in the world for a boy with dreams. You had dreams one time, too, Simeon."

Rashly, he waved her off. "Don't go throwin' that back at me."

She set her knitting down and rose to face him. "I remember when we bought this farm. You were full to poppin' of dreams, then."

Simeon huffed. No point dodging the truth of that. "I made my dream real, Ellen. Wide awake. That there's the diff'rence."

"So did John," she said. "But he couldn't do it here in Hinsdale. Nobody here buyin' graphic art in these parts."

"That don't excuse him runnin' off. Not when we needed him." The ache of John's leaving knotted in Simeon. "My Daddy said it right. It's only fools that can't find work where their loved ones are."

Ellen pinched her lips together as she shook her head. After snatching her knitting up, she sent a penetrating glance his way. "I can't see cuttin' another boy off, just 'cause he doesn't dream your dream."

David sat on John Holly's too-tall bed. Hard as he tried he couldn't help the tears that welled, then ran down his cheeks.

What was he to do now?

Mr. and Mrs. Holly had barely said a word to him since he saved Mr. Streeter's tree. But there'd been no shortage of words to each other. About him. As forcefully as Mr. Holly made his points, David couldn't help but overhear. Till Mrs. Holly closed the window.

Mr. Holly didn't want him. And that seemed all there was to it.

Footsteps sounded.

David wiped his face.

Mrs. Holly poked her head in. "Can I get you anything before you turn in?"

He shook his head. The last thing he wanted to do was to make life harder for Mrs. Holly. No harder than it already seemed to be.

She wandered up to his bedside, then handed him a tissue from her pocket. "Blow your nose good, now. You'll feel better."

Mrs. Holly was right. It did feel better to get all that out of his head. He balled up the used tissue and deposited it onto her extended palm. "I was out of tune with the Orchestra today. Wasn't I?"

Compassion shone in her eyes. "Oh, David..."

"I was. And now he doesn't want me."

She put a comforting arm around David's shoulders. "I don't think it's so much being in or out of tune. I guess you and Mr. Holly, well, it's like you're both sort of...on a different song." For a moment she just stood there. "Know what I think?"

David searched her face. "What?"

Mrs. Holly came around and perched on the bed across from him. "I think a boy smart as you—with talent like you've got—maybe you're bound for other places anyway."

Hope sparked in his spirit. Maybe this was all part of what Daddy had said. About going into the beautiful world. "You mean like one of those schools where I could get a start? Where I could study music?"

"Well," she said, "those schools take money. More than we'll ever see. But maybe when you're older you'll get there somehow."

David straightened, a thought burning in his mind. Even if Mrs. Holly didn't know about it, he had all those gold coins stashed away behind John Holly's dictionary. The ones Daddy told him to hide. Could they be his start? Carefully, David chose his words. "But if I had money, then you're saying I could go to the world and study?"

Her lips broke into a wistful smile. "Lotta things we'd all do if we had money." She patted his knee. "But, tell you what. Why don't you climb under those covers quick like? You can close your eyes tight. And you can dream about whatever you want to dream all night long. That don't cost a cent." She pulled back the covers and helped him climb under. Once he'd gotten settled, she brushed his forehead with a kiss. Just like Daddy used to.

"Goodnight, Mrs. Holly."

"Sleep sweet, Love." She snugged the covers up around his neck. "Mornin' will be here 'fore you know it. You put in a good bit of time choppin' and we'll see if Mr. Holly don't think better of things."

13

Jack Gurnsey ran a razor across his jaw line, then swished the shaving cream off in the sink.

His sister perched on the bathroom counter, massaging behind her kitten's ears.

Jack angled his head to trim the stubble off his sideburns. "I won't be gone long, Julia. You can stay with Miss Somers."

Julia almost spat. "You must be kidding. It's summer vacation. Do you seriously expect me to hang out with my schoolteacher?"

Predictable enough. Charlotte owed him a favor, though he cringed to ask. "How about you try Stacy Pepper, see if you can stay with her?"

"Cats make her eyes swell. I can stay by myself for one day."

"Nice try." He splashed some water on his face, then patted it dry with a towel. "You can come with me. Ride the train."

She tossed him a perturbed look. "And watch you do research all day? There's a thrill."

"You used to think so."

"Like when I was five." Julia hopped down off the bathroom counter. "Sometimes I used to stay at Sunnycrest. When Miss Grace lived there."

Jack hung up his towel. How could he discreetly curb this line of conversation, without letting on too much about the complexities with Barbara? He reached for a bottle of aftershave. "Well, I wouldn't impose on Ms. Holbrook. Not while she's just settling back in."

Not too hard to read the look on Julia's face. She wasn't buying it. Not for a second. "Why do you call her *Ms.* anyway? Miss Grace showed me your pictures with her from when you were kids."

"That was a very long time ago." He dabbed the soothing liquid onto his neck.

"Sure looked to me like you two used to be, kind of...a thing." That prying gaze of Julia's just wouldn't let go.

As nonchalantly as Jack could, he bobbed his shoulders. "Some people, you see them again, doesn't matter how long it's been. It's just instant between you. Like no time has passed."

He stowed his aftershave in the medicine cabinet. "Used to be like that with Ms. Holbrook, but now...not so much. I look at her and—to tell you the truth—I just don't know her anymore."

Julia grunted. "You think it's because she's so rich now?"

"I don't know," Jack said. "It's just...kind of a shame. That's all." A crying shame, for sure. Not that he'd elaborate more with Julia. But as much as he regretted what had come and gone with Barbara, he might as well get used it. They were neighbors in name only. Technically near. Yet for reasons beyond his imagining, worlds apart in spirit.

Simeon and Perry sputtered along through the cornfield on the harvester. Barely two rows of corn in the hopper, and already the thing lurched and pinged and clunked something awful.

Simeon tightened his jaw at the heavens. "Not now."

Perry urged the harvester on. "Come on, Old Girl."

"No use sweet talking farm machinery, Perry. Not as far as I can see." As if the thing had heard him, it let out a sickening scrape, then stopped cold as ice mid row. "Blast it! Of all the times."

"Lemme see." Perry jumped off and went to check out the engine. That Perry, he never gave up. Plenty of reason to or not.

Simeon groaned. How many times could Perry jerry-rig the old harvester? How long could they run the contraption on hopes and prayers? One more season. One last crop to pay off Streeter's note.

Usually, Simeon left matters of faith to Ellen. This was all Simeon had asked of the Lord in a very long time. Didn't seem so unreasonable a request. But apparently, the Almighty didn't see it Simeon's way. No, God looked down from heaven and flat ignored his petition. Right when he needed it most.

Perry continued to tinker with the engine, but Simeon didn't see the point. Sometimes dead was dead, and this was one of those times. He hopped off the harvester and trudged toward the house.

Outside, David swung his axe, determinedly working on that woodpile of theirs. Trying to make up for yesterday's fiasco with Streeter's tree, no doubt. Where did the kid think that wood in their pile had come from anyway? A tree. One that didn't have some crazy orphan kid campaigning to save it, not the way David saved Streeter's. Nothing about that boy staying there made sense. So, why did every swing of David's axe chip away at Simeon's bent to get rid of him?

SIMEON HUNG UP THE KITCHEN PHONE. Why he'd let Ellen talk him into even calling Charlie Pepper's farm equipment place, he couldn't figure. Like they'd float him a loaner in this economy.

Ellen dried her hands on her apron. "What about George? Maybe he would—"

Simeon raised a stifling hand. "George ain't gonna lend his new harvester to me. I'm his competition."

"You're his neighbor. You can try," Ellen replied.

"We ain't livin' in no Amish country, Ellen." Simeon rooted around for their phone directory. "This is free enterprise. Every man for himself. No bunch o' goody-gum-drops neighbors gonna come an' bail me out." He set David's father's violin case aside to look behind it on the shelf.

Of course, that would be the exact moment David decided to wander in the kitchen door, fresh from his chores at the woodpile. And the last thing Simeon needed was to get the boy going again about missing his daddy.

Too late though.

The boy cast a bittersweet eye on his father's violin. "I finished a lot of chopping, Mr. Holly."

"Yeah, I saw. That ought to do you for the day." Mr. Holly motioned toward the old violin. "Perry brung that down from the hay loft. Don't look like much, but he thought you might want it. Seein' as it was your Daddy's."

David ran his fingers across his father's battered case. "Maybe I'll take Daddy's violin out today. Would you like to go on a walk with me, Mr. Holly?"

"No, I don't want to go on a walk!" He spun back toward his wife. "Where'd you put the phone book, Ellen?"

Ellen pulled the book from the pantry and handed it to Simeon. She patted David. "It's not a good time, David. You run on. Enjoy yourself."

Still, David lingered.

Simeon flipped through the business pages for the number. "Rentin's gonna run me short, but what else am I to do? Let that crop o' mine rot on the stalks?"

Ellen turned his way. "Maybe you could get an extension."

"You think it makes one hoot o' matter to Streeter that this is my last payment? You think he don't want this land back?"

As David slipped out with the violin, Perry came in. Not a good sign in Simeon's book. Perry shut the door behind the boy. "Ain't no patchin' her up, I'm afraid. Gone this time."

Simeon scratched his head. "Take the truck and what we got to market. Least see what we can get for that little bit o' nothin'."

SIMEON FUMED. A visit to Charlie Pepper's farm equipment store hardly seemed worth the gas to drive there. Leastways, it got Ellen off his back. And he didn't mind the chance to clear his head from those crazy notions—about keeping David around.

Charlie guided Simeon by gear tasty enough to make any farmer salivate. Shiny as they came, even high tech, this stuff. A far cry from that bucket of bolts Perry couldn't patch for their crop. Figured. Not like that old harvester owed him anything. It had been used when he first bought it. But decades had passed between then and now. And how could he complain that it had finally plucked its last ear of corn? Just rotten timing, that's all.

Charlie walked Simeon right past the top-of-the-line harvester. As if Simeon could afford it. Still, Simeon eyed the thing long and hard.

"This one'd do ya right good," Charlie said. "State-of-the-art beaut' right there. Last of the lot."

Simeon ran his hand across the gleaming green paint. That engine untarnished by ages of wear. What he wouldn't give to have a gorgeous machine like this. But not a moment passed before reality struck. "I expect she runs right high."

Charlie slapped Simeon's shoulder. "Gotta keep up with the gear, Holly. Or get left behind. Most everybody else's corn is in already."

Simeon mulled it over. True enough, what Charlie said. Farmers all over had beat him to market. Envy curdled in his stomach. Hard as he'd worked, he couldn't figure it. Why them and not him?

Ellen always tried to put some kind of spiritual spin on these things. Not that he cottoned to that. No amount of pie-in-the-sky supposing changed a thing. Facts were facts. He'd need a bank loan to pull off buying a new harvester. Loans took collateral. Collateral Simeon didn't have. Not even close.

Asking for charity from the likes of Charlie Pepper—well, that kind of thing twisted up inside Simeon like an old phone cord. Maybe because posing that question he'd promised Ellen he would ask meant admitting something to Charlie. That he just couldn't swing it on his own.

He needed help.

Simeon chewed at his cheek. Shouldn't be so hard to get those few words out. Let Charlie turn him down, just like the Almighty had. And that would be that. He could go home and tell Ellen he'd done everything he'd promised.

He choked back the gathering moisture in his throat. Once more, he looked over the harvester—as if that jewel glimmering before him weren't exactly what he wanted. "So, Charlie. I don't know if I'm crazy 'bout all them bells and whistles. What do you s'pose it would take for a trial run? Maybe a short term rental?"

Barbara Holbrook fidgeted at her desk. Why couldn't she get comfortable there in that imposing library? Not like she hadn't grown up in that place, escaping into its many volumes.

She turned back to the spreadsheet on her laptop. Keeping up financial records gave her no thrills. But somebody had to manage all that money, and no one else remained to do it.

Tina stretched from a stepladder, hanging freshly washed drapes. "Hmm. Look at that. There's that boy. The one that went up to the organ on Sunday. Wandering in your garden with a fiddle."

Barbara rose to take a gander. Anything to avoid another moment wrestling with that spreadsheet.

Tina descended the stepladder. "You want me to run him off?"

She watched as the boy raised his violin over her roses, then launched into a run on the strings. Indeed, it was that orphaned boy, David, whose father lay buried in her cemetery. "No. Thank you, Tina. I'll go."

Even as Barbara left the house and crossed the yard, the boy never stopped playing that hauntingly beautiful melody. Instead, he seemed captivated at the sight of a fragrant blossom, opening in the sunlight. That *Double Delight* had always been her favorite. No matter how many times she took in its aroma, each new bud called her back again.

Barbara feigned a cough to make her presence known.

Finally, the boy looked up, his eyes shining.

"So then," she said. "Would you be so kind to tell me what the meaning of this is?"

David regarded her matter-of-factly. "But I was just telling you, only you didn't let me finish."

She furrowed her brow. "Telling me?"

"Yes, with Daddy's violin. Couldn't you understand?"

"Well..." In a way, she did.

"You looked as if you could." He tucked the instrument under his arm.

Barbara closed the distance between them. "You're David, aren't you?"

"Yes." He pointed down the walk. "I came down that stone path. I didn't know there was a place in the valley anywhere near this lovely."

"Didn't you?" A smile slipped across her lips. This David seemed much more educated than she had supposed. Almost a traveler from another time, when children were raised as she had been, to appreciate the beauty of creation. To speak with some measure of gentility. "Have you condescended to visit my garden?"

David gazed around. "I never found anything like this. Or like you, my Lady of the Roses."

Barbara suppressed a chuckle. "Very prettily put, Sir. But you should know that I am no Lady of the Roses. I am Ms. Holbrook, and I'm not in the habit of receiving unannounced gentlemen callers."

Undaunted, David turned toward the sundial by her reflecting pool. He ran his hand across the burnished bronze dial. "What is this?"

"It's a sundial," she said. "It marks the time."

David studied the Latin inscription, reading it aloud. "*Horas non numero nisi serenas.* I count...no hours but...unclouded ones."

Barbara felt her jaw slacken. "You read Latin?"

"Yes," he nodded. "But...what do you think this means?"

All her life, she'd grown up with that sundial in the garden, but not once had she thought about its inscription. "Well, I guess...what it says." She gestured toward the shadowed sliver on the dial. "It counts its hours by the shadow the sun casts. No sun, no shadow. So, only the sunny hours are counted by the dial."

The boy's face lit up. "Oh, I like that! I'd like to be like that, too, you know? Today, something in me keeps shining so much that they've all counted. But wouldn't it be great to just forget about all the hours when the sun didn't shine inside us? And only remember the nice ones?"

For a moment his thought disarmed her. But just as quickly, bittersweet memories sank in her soul. "Yes, I suppose if I had my way I'd forget quite a lot...actually all of my hours these days."

David looked at her, pleadingly. "Oh, Lady of the Roses, you don't mean... You can't mean that you don't ever have any sun."

She averted her gaze, swallowing the rising lump in her throat. "I mean that...I guess I'd hoped this one thing would happen. But it hasn't and..." There seemed no use going down that road with the boy. Involuntarily, her eyes misted. "What am I..." She straightened her back. "I hope you understand, but I do need to go, David. I have things to do. And you'd best be on your way."

Disappointment hung on the boy. "But—"

"Goodbye, David." Abruptly, Barbara turned. As quickly as she could, she retreated to the house and closed the door.

How David did it, she couldn't say. Somehow—intentionally or not—he'd made her lower her guard. Maybe all that lyrical language of his set her drifting back toward times gone by. Perhaps it was just one of those cloudy days, when she let things get to her.

Only one thing seemed quite clear, though. Another moment and that boy would have seen straight through her. The desolation of her spirit would have been laid completely bare.

Barbara set a hand across her chest to still its pounding. If she didn't protect that heart of hers, no one else would.

14

As dank as the precinct got, something about the sights and smells of the urban police station invigorated Jack. Funny, how much even this *pro bono* errand in the city buoyed his self-esteem.

Like somehow, he still mattered.

Lots of new faces around. Plenty of turnover in staff over the past couple of years since Jack had left the downtown sprawl. But thankfully, the old desk sergeant, Rudy, still gave him a reasonably friendly greeting. Until Jack asked for that favor.

Rudy shook that ageing mug of his. "Don't normally call in this kind of marker. I mean, come on, Gurnsey. What am I supposed to do? Not like you even practice here no more."

Jack leaned closer. "You've got kids yourself, Sarge. Think if something happened to you, okay? Wouldn't you want an old friend to cut you some kind of a break?"

The desk sergeant tapped his pen on as he mulled it over.

"Look, I know it's a long shot," Jack said. "But David seems like a good kid. Maybe somebody's looking for him. I don't know. What would it hurt to let me take a quick look?"

"You've been watching too much TV, Jack. No such thing as a quick look, little as you got to go on. And anybody logs onto this thing, it's gotta be me."

Jack lowered his voice as a cop passed. "You used to be a detective, Sarge. First grade, if I recall."

Rudy's smile collapsed. "Till the young pups squeezed me out. Spun this nothing bit of a desk job as a promotion."

"Seems to me they'd appreciate experience," Jack replied. "All those years of know-how you've got. You're still a detective inside."

"Yeah," Rudy said. "Enough to know you're snowing me."

Jack chuckled. "A little, I guess. But you can't tell me that something in you doesn't itch over a case like this. I mean, I don't get why a violinist—one who plays like his son says he did—why would he raise a prodigy alone on a mountaintop?"

"You said the mother died. Grief can do a real number on some people. Could've wigged clear outta his mind."

"That's just it," Jack answered. "He seemed really tired. Probably sick. But nothing in him struck me as mentally ill. And the boy, he might not have any street smarts, but he's been home-schooled. He's very articulate, far beyond his ten years. Doesn't anything in that seem compelling to you?"

Rudy checked around, but no one in the busy station seemed to be paying them much mind. "How far back are we talking?"

Jack relaxed his stance. "Maybe eleven years max."

The sergeant drew his computer keyboard closer. "Lotta missing person's cases in that time." He tapped in his password.

"I'll owe you one, Rudy."

Rudy studied his computer screen. "Oh, yeah. You betcha you will."

JACK FIDGETED. The Sarge sure hadn't exaggerated the volume of files. There'd been no point in limiting the search to the immediate region. And the national database teemed with hits that included the name *David*. This would take a while.

"Another David." Rudy grunted. "A last name would sure help. The mother's name. Whatever."

"All I've got is that first name. David. And that they both played the violin." The opportunity to ask more had been right there that night he picked the two of them up. Jack tortured himself. Why hadn't he taken more of an interest when he could have?

The Sarge looked mildly perturbed. "Course, no missing person report—no file, you know?"

Hope waning, Jack massaged the kink in his neck. This hunch had seemed a lot more reasonable a couple of hours ago. But then again, how could he bring himself to stop halfway after he'd come this far? How could he let an orphan down, just because he'd tired of searching? Nope. His adoptive parents had hung in there for him when the going got tough. And he would do exactly the same.

Jack renewed his resolve. As long as Rudy kept going, Jack would stand there with him. No matter how hungry he got or how long it took. He grabbed his cell from his pocket. No way he'd make it back to pick up Julia at Charlotte's. "You mind if I make a call while you do that?"

In between rhythmic keystrokes, Rudy eyed him. "Just keep it down, will ya?"

"Yeah, no problem." Jack scrolled his contacts to Charlotte's number. How many rings would the woman take to pick up? Not like he could leave a message for this kind of thing.

"Hello?" Charlotte cleared a frog in her throat.

Jack cupped his hand over the phone. "Hi, Charlotte. It's me, Jack."

"Julia's just fine, Jack. If I can assume she's why you called. We're up to our ears in gardening right now."

Jack grimaced. Oh, how he hated to impose more than he already had. "Any chance Julia can stay with you overnight? Checking this thing out has gotten a little more involved than I'd thought."

Charlotte paused a moment.

"Look, if it's too much trouble, I'll—""

"No, no," she said. "I suppose that's fine. And I won't say I told you so."

Julia's voice bled through in the background. "Is that Jack?"

"It's your big brother, all right," Charlotte said, her voice coming through the receiver. "I told him you could stay the night. Wipe your hands, Julia."

"Charlotte, I can't really talk much—"

Julia picked up with a hushed tone. "This better be supremely, outstandingly important, Bro."

Jack smiled. "I seem to recall you owe me one. On account of letting you keep a certain stray kitten, named Sally."

Julia sputtered back a whisper. "Well, you should know—Miss Somers—she's pretty much decided I'm her personal slave. I already weeded half her stupid yard."

Charlotte chirped audibly in the background. "Goodness, Child. This is a peony and the roots are completely... How long has this been exposed?"

A world-class huff sounded through the phone. "It was just...wait a minute," Julia said, apparently to Charlotte.

"Julia?"

"One night, Jack," Julia replied. "Then, with or without you, me and Sally are going back home." With a click, Julia was gone.

Jack watched Rudy dig through a veritable avalanche of computer hits. It could be a long night. With no promise that a needle hid anywhere in this haystack.

Hinsdale's old train station fascinated David, its crisscrossed tracks stretching out across the valley floor. Such a sight. Even more so up close this way. A young family boarded a passenger car, wheeling small suitcases behind them. Teenagers hopped off, slinging backpacks over their shoulders. At the near side of the track, a matronly woman stood at a booth, exchanging money for a ticket.

David approached the man at the ticket window, his mouth open in amazement. This was just like Daddy had described, only so much grander.

The man in the window looked over the top of his glasses. "Traveling alone?"

"Not just yet, Sir. But can you tell me—does this train go to the world where the music schools are?"

A puzzled look came over the man's face as another boy's voice broke through.

"Hey, Geek-bait. Goin' somewhere?" Eugene Streeter and his gang of boys smirked David's way.

"Yes," David replied. "One day, I am."

Eugene didn't look so convinced.

"I'm going to go out to the world," David added. "Where I can study."

The boys howled.

David smiled. Maybe they liked him better than he'd thought.

Eugene stepped closer, an innocent look on his face. "Well, isn't that just the sweetest thing you ever heard, Asa?"

Asa rolled his eyes. "School's out for summer, Wack-a-doo."

"Asa, give the kid a chance." Eugene scratched under his chin as he looked David over. "You know, maybe we got off on the wrong foot. You said your name's David, right?"

"That's right."

Eugene cracked his knuckles. "So, David. Maybe, I could teach you a thing or two." A grin snaked across his lips.

David searched Eugene's expression. The words seemed nice enough. Maybe they could be friends after all. "You could?"

"Yeah." Eugene exchanged a look with Asa, before turning back to David. "You wanna learn to play a game?"

Something bubbled up inside David. "You mean baseball?"

"Tell you what, Davey-boy," Eugene said. "You catch on quick to this first little game of ours. Then, we'll see about baseball."

DAVID CAUGHT HIS BREATH after running to the town square. Eugene had said to follow him and the other boys there, so that's what David did. Not easy keeping up with his violin in tow, but David ran as fast as he could.

A lanky man left the grocery market. He took a long drink from what looked like a bottle with a brown paper bag crunched around it.

"Luke Dowd." Eugene grinned. "Awesome." Eugene motioned the boys to crouch just around the corner. "Stay back." He pulled a coil of wire from his pocket and extended one end to Asa.

Apparently, Asa already knew how to play this game. He ran across the sidewalk, stretching out the curls in the wire, then he ducked low on the other side.

Eugene handed his end of the wire to David. "Now, you hold this end. Keep it low and real tight. Flat to the ground till I give the signal."

David's brow furrowed. "This is part of the game?"

Eugene slapped David's shoulder. "That's right, Davey. Part of the game. Then, we play baseball."

That man shuffled precariously down the walk. Eugene counted down with his fingers. Just as the man neared the wire, Eugene gave the signal and Asa raised his end of the wire, right in front of the man.

Frantic, David whispered to Eugene. "But that's going to make him—"

Asa yanked the wire higher on his side. Enough to send the man reeling. The bag hit the cement with crack of breaking glass, its contents gushing out.

In a flash, Eugene, Asa, and the other boys sprinted off.

Agape, David held the wire in one hand and Daddy's violin in the other.

Luke Dowd rolled over on the pavement and called after the escaping boys. "Yeah, you little thugs. You'd better run!"

Fear gripped David's heart. What would that man think? He dropped the wire and darted through passing townsfolk. Checking back only heightened David's distress.

The angry man had already lumbered unsteadily to his feet. No longer did the other boys have his attention. They'd already disappeared. Instead, he narrowed his gaze at David.

David bolted away, just as fast as his legs would carry him. Long-repressed memories invaded his heart-seizing reality.

Only four-years-old again. Weaving through a horde of foot traffic in a darkly looming city.

A quick look back confirmed David's present plight. The man fought his way after him, through everyone in his path.

Gasping, David careened into Eugene's father as he exited the Post Office.

"Hey!" Mr. Streeter's packages went flying. "Watch it!"

David veered into the next alley. There had to be someplace to hide. Familiar flashes taunted his memory.

A dark alley, flanked by towering buildings.

No way out. Nowhere to hide.

Except that dumpster, filled with stinking garbage.

Panic gripped David. No place to hide in Hinsdale's alley either. Not even a dumpster. But thankfully, the alley opened onto another street in the back.

David raced through. He flattened himself against the back wall of the grocery store. Heaving for air, he scanned the run-down houses butted up against one another across the street. Paint peeled door-to-door. Trash littered the pavement. What porches existed sagged forlornly. Odd how close to the inviting town square this ramshackle bunch of houses stood.

He dashed across the street and ducked behind the shelter of an old, ripped sofa at the curb. For a long while, he fixated back on the alley. No sign of the man he'd accidentally had a part in tripping. Maybe he'd given up. Slowly, David's pulse settled into a normal rhythm.

Daddy's violin looked okay, despite all the bobbling of the run. But where had he found himself? A bleary-eyed man slouched on his stoop, downing the contents of a cellophane bag, while grousing with a filthy-looking woman.

"Git outta here. Scat!" The woman yelled.

"You mean me?" David pointed to himself.

"Yeah, you. Go on, git! Nothin' to see here."

Quickly, David rose. He meandered along with Daddy's violin. How he wished inspiration would strike, but how could it in this place? He paused in front of a dilapidated little house with the name *Glaspell* scrawled on a dented mailbox. Faded children's laundry dangled limply on a clothesline.

David ran an affectionate hand across the scroll of Daddy's violin as he gazed at the tiny dwelling. "It's not so beautiful, is it? But Daddy said we could make it beautiful if we will." David closed his eyes for a moment. He raised Daddy's violin and began to play. A lovely strain came forth, in stark contrast to his dreary surroundings.

How long he kept playing, David didn't know. That's the way it had always been with music, the way it transported him to another place and time.

A small hand tapped his shoulder, bringing his melody to a halt. David opened his eyes to see a skinny girl there.

She opened a grimy palm with a coin on it. "I'm Betsy Glaspell. My brother, Joe, in there... He said to give you this quarter."

David blinked. What was this? Money? "I don't understand. Why would he want me to take that?"

"He wants you to come in," Betsy said, "an' keep on playin' a while. He'd give you more, but he don't have it."

"You mean your brother, Joe..." David's eyes widened. "You're saying he likes it?"

Betsy led David into their humble abode. By the window, sat a small boy. So gaunt and pale.

The boy turned at the slap of the screen door. "Is he coming, Betsy? Will he play?"

"Yes, I'll play, Joe," David said. "I'm the one."

"Come over here," the boy said.

His curiosity piqued, David approached.

Joe lifted a hand. "And will you let me touch the fiddle? Ain't nobody home, just Betsy and me."

He looked around. "Well, sure." Tentatively, David extended Daddy's violin to Joe.

Gently, Joe stroked the wood and ran his fingers over the strings. Almost like he could hear the music inside.

"This one's my father's." David couldn't help but smile. Finally, someone appreciated Daddy's instrument. He released it into Joe's hands.

Joe raised it to his nostrils and drew in the scent. "Mama said my daddy used to play in a jazz band. He played a big old bass. Bigger 'n me."

Betsy set a fist on her hip. "Liar. You ain't got no daddy."

Joe whipped toward her. "Do, too."

"Joe..." David did his best to sort the situation out in his racing mind. "Did you understand what I was playing out there? Could you see it? Like the cloud-boats in the sky. And my silver river in the valley. And the wind in the trees. The little brook going off to the far country?"

Betsy scowled. "I told you, Joe, he's crazier 'n a corn puff. Everybody says it."

"No, Betsy." Joe shook his head. "I think I do understand." He turned in David's direction. "You mean, inside you. You see those things. Then, you try to make the fiddle say what you see. Is that it?"

David's spirit soared. "You do understand. You see it, too?"

Betsy flipped her wrist with a laugh. "Joe don't see nothin'. He's blind."

David studied the boy in the window's stark backlight. "You mean you really can't see anything? Nothing at all?"

"Not with my eyes," Joe said. "But can you play again?"

Wonder filled David's chest. Going through Eugene Streeter's dirty trick hadn't been fun. But somehow, something good had come out of it.

Running away had led him to where he seemed meant to be—inside this little house. To a blind boy who longed to see everything David could show him.

With Daddy's violin at his chin, David decided. He would show Joe Glaspell all he knew of the beautiful world, everything that burst from his soul. It would be that beautiful work meant for him today. And all the way off in the far country, Daddy would be so pleased he had found it.

15

Simeon Holly secured the canvas tarp over the load in the back of his truck. They couldn't afford to loose a single ear of that Silver Queen. Not this time. He tied the cord tight, then raised a glistening arm to his brow. No point in wiping the sweat off with his sleeve, not the way his clothes had soaked through.

The kitchen door slapped closed. Ellen headed his way, a tall glass of ice water in her hand.

Spent, Simeon waved her off. How could he stop and rest, what with Perry still working so hard in the field?

For a while, Ellen just stood there, extending the refreshment. "If you won't eat, drink something. You get yourself dehydrated, then where will we be? Heat stroke, no less."

Condensation beaded outside the glass. In a thirsty gulp, Simeon downed the whole thing. Plain water never tasted so good.

Ellen shielded her eyes from the setting sun. Far across the field, she gazed toward Perry as he steered the rented harvester down yet another row. "Did you at least ask Perry if he wanted dinner? Not like he has a wife to fix for him."

"Course, I asked, Ellen." He handed the glass back. "Much as you might think so, I ain't no ogre."

"I know."

"Perry wanted to press on, too," Simeon said. "He knows 'less we get this crop to market quick, I can't pay him neither. He's got plenty ridin' on this, too."

The load of it all weighed heavy on Simeon's shoulders. What more could he do than he'd already tried to save their farm? And still that sickening sense of dread crept through his innards. How could they have come this far and still draw up short? He ran his hand across the boards wrapped around his truck bed. "Remember when I built these rails?"

An empathetic glint lit in Ellen's eyes. "I recall dinner spoiled. Never could quit nothin' till it's done." She pointed toward the truck's cab. "I remember when John painted your name and that ear of corn there on the door for you, too."

Simeon slumped against the truck. "It's over, Ellen. Gotta face up. I give it all I got. And I guess all just ain't doin' it."

Somehow, she managed a smile. "I don't know. We still got us."

"Yeah. Just you an' me." For some odd reason, David's young face flashed in Simeon's mind. He let out a groan. Might as well speak his piece to Ellen. She'd read him like a book anyhow. "No way they're gonna let us keep fosterin' David, you know. Not now."

Ellen peered back with doe-like astonishment. "You were thinking... I mean, we—"

Simeon shrugged. "You ain't no more surprised 'bout it than I've been. Ever since we talked to that social worker from county. Just keeps poppin' in my head. How much I'd miss the little fella. No matter what I said."

Her eyes glistened. Looked like she'd miss David, too.

With a sigh, Simeon scanned the property. Defeat stared back. All those years, he'd tilled that soil. And to what end? "You an' me's one thing, Ellen. We'll make out somehow. But all this land, this work... I s'pose if it ain't for somebody, then I don't know what."

Quietly, Tina peered into Sunnycrest's stately master bedroom. Barbara still stood there at the window, overlooking the creek. Sadness had hung so thick in the air, ever since Barbara chased that boy, David, off the property.

But what could Tina do? She couldn't bring Grace Holbrook back to cheer her niece. Would that she could have. And she couldn't make heads nor tails of what had gone wrong between Barbara and Jack Gurnsey. But a woman didn't stare out the window at a man's house like that for nothing.

Tina cleared her throat. "Excuse me."

"Oh." Barbara turned. "I didn't realize you were there."

"Yes, I..." She motioned downstairs toward the dining room. "The table's set and dinner's coasting in the oven. Whenever you're ready for it."

Barbara exhaled wearily. "To be frank, I don't have much of an appetite. Thank you, though." She wandered from the turret, back into the room. "You heading out?"

Tina nodded. "Betsy said she'd get supper started for Joe. But I'd best get back and help her. It's a lot to put on a girl her age."

"How old is she, again?"

"Twelve. But twelve...it's not what twelve used to be for us. Sure grow up fast these days."

"That they do." A wistful sheen reflected in Barbara's eyes. "I don't know why I hurried that boy, David, off earlier. His father was right there, buried not fifty yards away and I completely..." She emptied her lungs. "Do you think I should have taken him to the grave?"

Tina wrung her hands. "Ms. Holbrook—"

"It's Barbara, remember?"

"Barbara." More than once now, permission had been given. So, why did it take everything Tina had in her to be that familiar?

"I should have walked him over there." Barbara sat on the bed. "I should have been brave enough to show him where his father is. Don't you think?"

Tina's mind swam. What if her opinion would make Barbara feel worse than she already did? She steadied herself on the doorjamb. "To be honest, I'm not sure it's my place to tell you what to—"

"Your place?" Barbara studied her, like she could see clean through her. "You need to know something, Tina. I don't think of you as an underling. There's no caste system here. You work for me. I pay you. That makes us even. Equals in my book."

"Yes, well..." Tina smoothed her apron.

"And as my peer, I'd like to know what you'd have done." Barbara waited what seemed forever.

Tina mulled things over. "I can't say I know for sure. Not like I was on the spot all of a sudden, the way he had you."

"No. I guess not."

She braved a step closer to her employer. It seemed like crossing a line, but on the other hand, she'd been welcomed. Maybe something she could say would help Barbara. Somehow.

Tina reached beyond herself for words. Then—just like that—there they came. Like all she had to do was open her mouth and know that He would fill it. "Stuff like this happens and, to tell the truth, it makes me miss your Aunt Grace. Even if she didn't have an answer right off to whatever had my head tangled up in knots, she always said she'd pray about it. And she did."

Barbara shook her head fondly. "I'm not near the saint she was."

Tina chuckled. "I used to tell her that, too. Especially when I'd made a royal mess of things. Then, your auntie, she'd just brush it off like it was nothing. She'd say I should stay on the alert. Keep these eyes and this heart of mine open. See if the good Lord would give me another chance, another go at it. To make it all right."

A nostalgic smile brightened Barbara's face. "A divine do-over, she called it. Yeah, she said that to me, too. And I've needed one, more times than I admit to most people."

"Yeah, me too," Tina replied. Maybe she and Barbara weren't so different after all. Tina started to go, then turned back. "You remind me of her, you know?"

Barbara tipped her head. Almost as if she didn't believe it. "So ironic, Tina. I was just going to say the same thing about you."

TINA TRUDGED UP HER WALK. There sat Luke Dowd, slouched on her porch steps. Bruised. And fully lit.

Why did the guy have to keep drinking himself senseless? Of course, her parents had done the same thing. Just secretly, behind closed doors.

Funny, the roller-coaster life could be. One minute Tina could be soaking in a moment straight out of heaven. And the next, reality would smack her flat across the face. Or it would try to, Grace Holbrook would say. Only Tina shouldn't let it steal her peace of mind. And she wouldn't. Not tonight. Not ever again. She and Luke—they were over for good. Unless Luke found the way to his knees.

She fumbled for her house key. "You get into it with somebody?"

Luke combed his fingers through that raven mop of his. "Lousy kid. I'll remember him, though."

Tina set a hand on her hip. "How you gonna remember anything, drunk as you are?"

A screechy tone bled in through the window. Luke plugged his ears.

"Go on home, Luke. I'm sorry you got yourself hurt, but you can't keep comin' here. I got kids to feed and they don't need to be seein' you like this."

Luke let out a hoot. "Joe can't see me any which way. Boy's pitch-black blind."

The momma bear rose up in Tina. She leveled Luke with a glare. "That boy of mine sees more than you know. More than you seem to." As quickly as she could, she turned the key in the lock, slipped through the door and bolted it closed.

Luke pounded hard against the door from outside. "Ah, come on, Tina. Can't you take a joke?"

One way or another, Luke had a way of pushing her buttons. He'd turn his issues back on her, like he had no problem at all and she was some kind of killjoy. There'd be no point in lashing back or trying to get in one last zinger. Grace Holbrook's words rang in Tina's memory:

Shake the dust off. Walk away.

And that's exactly what Tina did. Step-by-step she released every last thread that tugged at her heart, everything that tied her to that dysfunctional excuse for a relationship. Whether or not there'd ever be another guy for her, she had to get over this one.

The scent of candied yams hit her nostrils. A glance into the kitchen confirmed that Betsy had dinner going. Across the living room, Joe lowered a well-worn violin, no doubt the source of that screeching she'd heard.

"Hi, Sweetie." Tina put her bag down. "Where'd you get that?"

A soft smile lightened Joe's face. "It's okay. A boy loaned it to me so I could try to see things with it."

Betsy leaned in from the kitchen. "It was that kooky orphan kid, David."

So the boy with the violin had been over here, too. Tina reached toward her son. "Mind if I take a look at that?"

With a seeming reluctance, Joe extended the instrument toward her. "Can I keep it, please? For a while?"

She checked the thing over. Skin oils from what looked like years of use blackened the wood in places. Must have been ages since the thing had been cleaned. "Well, it don't look like much," she said. "So...I suppose."

David wandered back toward the Hollys' house. Even from a distance, something just didn't seem right. For one thing, instead of heading out after a hard day's work in the field, Perry Larson sat slumped on the porch steps.

He caught the farmhand's eyes as he neared. "I thought you said you were going to play cards at the firehouse tonight."

Perry Larson shook his head. "That's what I thought, too. Nothin' to bet with, though. Sad state when it's just penny ante." He gestured toward the house. "I'd lay low in there, if I was you."

David sat beside him on the steps. "What do you mean?"

The man blew out a long breath. "Well, I s'pose I might as well tell you. Won't be a secret much longer." Again, he tipped his head toward the door. "They had a stroke o' bad timin', Mr. and Mrs. Holly did."

From the look on Perry Larson's face, this didn't seem good. "What happened?"

"I dunno if you'll make sense of it. Seeing' as money ain't somethin' you know." Perry Larson flicked some dirt off his jeans. "It's 'bout ten thousand dollars money they owed. Here, like this." He pulled a large silver coin out of his pocket. "This here's a silver dollar. You see lots o' paper bills along the way. But this here's the first silver dollar I ever made. I got it toting groceries, so I never spend it. Just keep it right here in my pocket."

"Every day?"

"Mmm-hmm," he said. "To remind me what can come if I work hard and keep this heart 'o mine right." Perry patted a hand against his chest. "But, just imagine yourself ten thousand of them silver dollars. Heaps and heaps. More 'n I ever seen in my life."

David peered up at the sky. "Like the stars."

"That's right." Perry turned the coin between his fingers. "An' that's how many of these things the Hollys owe to Streeter. By the end o' this week."

David studied the silver dollar.

"Pity." Perry hung his head. "The Hollys, they had it, too, all in that crop out there. Only the harvester give out and Mr. Holly, he had to spend it to rent. Plus it made us late. And the price o' corn dropped meantime, so..." Wistfully, he scanned the property. "Looks like Streeter's gonna get this land back, after all these years. Hate to see it."

"Well," David said, "can't Mr. Streeter wait?"

Perry Larson shook his head. "Streeter's been wantin' the extra land back for a while now. I expect he'll be takin' it over right off."

How could that be? David's mind whirled. "With them living here?"

"Sure. Only they'll have to pack up and get out, you know."

David blinked. "Well, isn't there something else...something to do?"

The farmhand just shrugged. "It's the way the world works, Boy. Might as well know." He raised that silver dollar again. "These things ain't sproutin' on corn stalks."

A frightening thought shook David to the core. He had those gold coins hidden away. The ones that Daddy gave him. Only he needed that gold to pay for his start. For his train ticket into the world and for the music schools he'd find there. Still, something inside told him to probe. "And you say...money, that would fix it?"

A smirk crossed Perry's face as he stared at his silver dollar. "Ten thousand o' them. That's what it'd take."

In a way, what Perry Larson said helped David release the tension building up in his chest. "You mean...that there wouldn't be anything else that would do. Only silver pieces like those?"

"Course there would. Money's money. Any kind would do it." The man tucked the silver dollar deep into his pocket.

David's face fell. Maybe his gold could work after all. He didn't have near ten thousand coins like Perry Larson said. But maybe it would help somehow. Out of nowhere, reluctance blanketed David's mind. How could he give up what Daddy had left him? David rose, the load heavy on his shoulders. Without another word, he shuffled toward the house.

Quietly, David padded through the living room, past the kitchen door. Mr. and Mrs. Holly sat in there, their backs to him. Mr. Holly hunched over, his head in his hands.

Mrs. Holly sniffled, then brushed away a tear. "Simeon, have you thought... We might...go to John. For help."

Mr. Holly's back straightened. His voice took on a rigid tone as he wagged a finger at her. "Ellen, you'd best understand here and now that I'd rather lose the whole thing and starve than ask a penny from John." He pushed off the chair to his feet.

David slipped to the steps and hurried up. He could only hope and pray Mr. Holly didn't know he'd listened in on what they'd said. Why Mr. Holly got so mad about the idea of going to his son, David couldn't imagine. But things sounded every bit as desperate as Perry Larson just said.

Alone in John Holly's room, David pushed the door shut. He set a hand over his beating heart and squeezed his eyes shut. But they popped back open, trained on that hiding place he'd chosen, behind John's dictionary. Maybe another look at the gold would help.

Ever so carefully, David drew Daddy's sack out of hiding. He carried it over to the too-tall bed and emptied out the coins. Sorrow overtook him as he ran his hands through the treasure. As soon as he thought about what Daddy would say, David knew. He had to give it up. All of it. After everything the Hollys had done for him, he had to do what he could to help them.

Still, regretful whispers couldn't help but slip out as David pored over the gold coins. "You're supposed to be my start. You're going to take me on the train, out to the music schools in the world. You're supposed to help me find my work." All good things. But maybe this was the beautiful work Daddy meant that he could do.

David wiped his face and gathered up every last coin into the sack. Slowly, he went down the stairs. Perry leaned against the kitchen doorway, his back to David.

Mr. Holly's voice sounded from inside. "No sense you stayin' on, Perry. I'll get what I owe you somehow."

Perry Larson chased away the notion with a wave. "Don' be worryin' about that now, hear? I ain't goin' nowhere. Bitter or not, we see this through together. All the way to the end."

David slipped to Perry's side. The Hollys turned toward him. "I've been thinking...that maybe I could help. About the money."

Perry patted his back. "Now, look-it here, Boy. This ain't your frame o' mind. It ain't about no floofy clouds or bluebird singin' or brooks runnin' off somewhere."

Mrs. Holly headed in David's direction. "Go on to bed, David. We'll talk in the morning."

"Go on," Perry said. "Mind Mrs. Holly."

David glanced between the grown ups. "But they gave me food and let me stay when nobody else would. And now I want to do something for them."

Mr. Holly turned David's way. "Listen to me, Boy. It's more 'n decent of you to want to do somethin'. But ain't nothin' nobody can do at this point. Nothin' but face facts."

David fished the sack from his pocket. He untied the strap and poured the gold out on top of the kitchen table. The coins clattered on the tabletop, but no one said a word. They just stared at the gold, their mouths hanging open.

"There aren't so many pieces," David said. "And they aren't silver like yours, Perry Larson. There's only one hundred and six. I counted."

Perry reached out and picked up a gold coin.

Mrs. Holly just stood there, her eyes pooling. "Simeon, look!"

Perry spread the coins. "A hundred and six?"

David winced. "I know you need ten thousand, but maybe they'd help some. Maybe they'd be a start." Though his voice broke a bit at the thought of his own lost start, David willed himself to smile.

Mr. Holly sat back down, speechless.

"Great snakes, Boy!" Perry ran his fingers through the gold. "Where'd you get all this?"

"From my daddy," David replied, "in the far country, you know. He gave it to me, before he left."

Mrs. Holly picked up a coin and squinted at it. "These date back to... Why, most of these are early 1800s. No telling what they're worth."

Dismay sunk David's spirit. "Won't they do?"

Mr. Holly leaned back, rubbing a hand over his jaw as he studied the gold from a distance. He didn't look nearly as excited as the others seemed to be.

Perry Larson turned to Mr. Holly. "Now, I ain't professin' to know much about the hand of the

Lord, but it do strike me that this gold here comes right near miraculous for you."

Simeon rose with a shake of his head. "The money is the boy's, Larson. It ain't mine."

Perry's jaw dropped. "He's givin' it to you."

Mr. Holly's expression soured. "An' how do we know where his daddy got it? Think on it. How did a homeless recluse get all that gold?"

Defensiveness straightened David's spine. Not for himself, but for Daddy. "I don't know, Sir. But I do know he didn't steal it. He said his daddy gave it to him, too."

Mr. Holly clenched his jaw for a moment, then turned to David, his face softening and hardening all at the same time. "You're a mighty fine boy to offer, David. But I just can't take it, that's all."

Simeon kicked off his shoes and tucked them beside the nightstand. From the corner of his eye, he watched as Ellen pulled down the covers. She didn't say a thing as she fluffed his pillow, but her silence echoed in his ears.

After all these years, the woman didn't have to utter a word. One look at her told him plenty. She didn't stand on his side of this decision. Once again, he had to seem the bad guy and stick up for doing what had to be done.

He stood at the bedside across from her. "David is nothing but a child, Ellen. He don't know what he's doing. He don't know nothing 'bout how valuable that gold is."

Ellen hardly raised her eyes. She just kept on smoothing those infernal covers, like she was some hotel maid. "I'm not sure what's more valuable to you, Simeon—that gold or your pride."

He clenched his fingers. "Got nothing to do with pride, Ellen."

"You know, Simeon..." Ellen looked up. "I spent most the day praying for some way out of this. Maybe this gold is it. It could be the answer."

Simeon inhaled. As usual, she'd spun this mess into something spiritual. "Maybe that's the diff'rence between us, Ellen. I learned long ago that you work your way outta things. Don't leave much time for prayin'."

"No time for prayin', huh?" Something fierce locked Ellen's misty gaze on his. "No time for loving or laughing or..." Disappointment flashed across her face.

"Oh, come on, Woman..."

"Work, work, work." She threw her hands out to her sides. "That's all you do, Simeon. So you can provide, and you can be the one that done it. And you can turn your back on living and me and your own son. Then you thumb your nose at a gift sent straight outta heaven—just as long as it makes you right."

Jack Gurnsey tapped at the downtown public library's computer keyboard. No one else had come to request the space, but the twenty-minute limit they'd given him had elapsed a good hour ago. And the rumble of that industrial-sized vacuum cleaner underscored the librarian's hint. He'd have to pack it in soon. Jack clicked on yet another of a series of search hits in the library's massive archives.

So many rabbit trails. Hours on end at the police precinct had only yielded an aching back and a nasty paper cut. Maybe David's father hadn't committed a crime. Or he hadn't been reported for one. Not so much as a single missing person's report tracked. But perhaps there would be something, somewhere in the library's newspaper archives. Some lead on anything that sounded like David. Anything with his first name and that keyword *violin*.

The janitor slowed beside him. "Closin' up in five minutes, hear?"

"Okay." Jack barely looked at the guy. "I'll wrap it up." He turned back to his screen and scanned a loading headline: *Dead Trail on Killer.*

Jack froze.

What was this?

Something collapsed in Jack. He sat forward, skimming through the five-year-old column for connections, murmuring aloud. "*David, David...*" In a moment, there it was:

A mention of a violinist.

The man's brutally murdered wife.

As Jack raced through the article, electricity coursed through his body. A single sentence leapt out:

> *There is still no sign of the father or his young son, David, who have not been seen since the night of the slaying.*

Jack sat back, thunderstruck.

16

Simeon Holly tromped down the kitchen steps, like any other morning. Only something different stirred inside. No getting around it. This day marked a turning point. In a way, it felt like stepping off a cliff, with nothing at all there to catch him. But one thing was for sure. There'd be no going back once he got up the gumption to do what needed to be done.

Out back of the barn, Perry started up the rented harvester and chugged it along toward the remaining corn crop. David swung an axe. Already the boy dutifully chopped their wood. Simeon stole a glance back at the kitchen door. Just like he thought, Ellen stood there watching as he neared David.

The boy cleared split pieces from the block. "Good morning, Mr. Holly. Did you see what a pretty day it is?"

Simeon balked. Truth was, he hadn't paid the weather a moment of mind. Not past the fact that the night's rain hadn't amounted to a tea cup. He took in the sky. "Yeah, pretty enough. I s'pose it is."

"You and Perry Larson going to bring in the rest of that corn?"

Simeon kicked the toe of his boot against the dirt. No telling why doing this seemed so blasted hard, but he might as well get on with it. That or he'd have Ellen to wrangle with about it. "Larson, he's gonna get things started, but I'm thinking, well..." He motioned back toward his wife. "Mrs. Holly and me—we wanted to know if you'd like to take us on one o' them walks."

SIMEON CRUNCHED DOWN THE FOREST PATH with Ellen. David scampered along just ahead of them, like a giddy young colt. Simeon volleyed his eyes toward Ellen.

She sent back a smirk. "No good being in the woods if your mind is back in your cornfield."

"All right, already." Couldn't get away with anything. Not with that wily woman. Somehow, she always knew.

Okay, then. Buckle down and focus on the here and now. Ticks crawlin' thick as thieves this time of year. He'd have to check up, down, and sideways once they got back. That and he'd see to Perry's progress. By afternoon, they ought to get that last load to market. So, was it too much to hope the price they'd get wouldn't drop again today?

Ellen poked him.

He let out a guilty grunt. How did she figure him out every time?

David beamed as he pointed out an old pine. "And do you see this tree—how the moss grows all green and wonderful just on this side?"

For David's sake, Simeon did his level best to take an interest. Anyhow, to pretend to. "I s'pose."

"Daddy said that moss, it's like a compass in the woods. It tells us which way is north so we don't get lost."

Ellen gave Simeon a tight-lipped nudge. "Isn't that something?"

"Oh, and look!" David pointed out a different clump of moss on yet another tree nearby. "This moss is special medicine kind of moss. Daddy showed me how to make him some tea with it and whenever he got sick it would always make him better. He made it for me once when I got sick, too."

"That's fine," Simeon said. "Just fine."

On and on they walked. As if working folks had all day for this kind of lollygagging. But then again, the notion that had kept Simeon up all night tossed around inside him. May as well put it out there so they could get on with the day. He cleared his throat. "I do believe you, Boy. About your daddy not stealin' that gold he give you. No boy like you comes off o' no thief."

David stopped in his tracks.

A new respect welled up in Simeon. Not that he'd expected to get all choked up, but something brimmed inside him. It thickened in his windpipe and misted in his eyes. "You're a good son, David. Good and loyal, and..." He exchanged a glance with Ellen, then turned back to David. "And I wish you was mine. I really do."

A blush came over David's face. "You do?"

Conviction swelled in Simeon. "Your daddy didn't steal that gold and I won't steal it neither," he said.

Ellen shot a concerned look his way.

"But I will use it," he said, "since you was so good to offer. Long as we're clear it's a loan, David. Strict by the books. And some day, God helpin', I'll be payin' it all back."

Ellen set her hand in the crook of his arm, like she used to. Back years and years ago.

He covered her fingers with his. "Meantime, the Mrs. and me, we called that woman at county, the one you was talkin' all that French with. We told her we're wantin' to be your foster folks. Long as you'd like it that way."

David's eyes pooled. "You want me?"

Simeon reached out and patted the boy's shoulder. "Certainly do. You're my boy."

Jack Gurnsey strode across the sun-dappled campus of a downtown Conservatory. Students moved across the quadrangle changing classes, many with instruments in tow. An accomplished string quartet rehearsed, seated on boulders under a copse of trees. Jack drew in the morning air.

Finally, everything made sense.

Being back in the city felt good. Especially now that Jack had found what he had. What energized him so? It didn't take long to pinpoint. For the first time in a long time, he actually felt like a man.

Purpose rose in Jack's spirit as he scaled the steps to a limestone administrative building. The secret he'd discovered danced inside. This Professor Stanton had no idea why he'd set up a last-minute meeting. What this woman would be like, he had no idea. But something in him had to be absolutely sure.

Before he revealed what he knew.

Any qualms Jack may have had vanished at Professor Stanton's sparkling smile and the warmth of her handshake. Though they'd never met, that lovely face of hers had traces of familiarity. Honey blonde hair hung loosely around her shoulders.

"Hello, Professor Stanton," he said. "Thanks so much for seeing me on such short notice. I'm Jack Gurnsey. An attorney from Hinsdale."

"Pleasure to meet you." She motioned toward a sofa and chair. "Why don't we sit?"

"Probably a good idea." Jack slipped a hand into his breast pocket as he followed her and they took their seats. There it was, that tiny framed photo of David's mother. His angel-mother, as David called her. "You're probably wondering why I've come."

"No one's suing me, I hope." She grinned.

"No, no. Nothing like that, but..." Jack took a comparative look at the photo before handing it to Professor Stanton. Uncanny, the resemblance. "I just wanted to show you a little something," he said. "Something that belongs to someone I know. A *pro bono* client of sorts."

A questioning expression crossed Professor Stanton's face as she accepted the photo. Then, at the sight of the image, her aqua eyes filled. "Oh, dear Lord. This is... It's Catherine. My sister." She searched Jack's face, clearly stunned. "Where did you get this?"

Assurance filled Jack. "From a ten-year-old boy. His name is—"

"David." A tear traced down the professor's cheek. "I never thought I'd see him again. He's my nephew."

Her cell at her ear, Barbara Holbrook checked a gold coin through a magnifying glass. Five minutes and counting on hold. Simeon and Ellen Holly waited patiently with David, across her desk.

Nearby, Tina busied herself, dusting the study's bookshelves, dutifully wiping each volume.

Simeon shifted in his chair. "Real sorry 'bout the short notice on this. But we thought since Ellen here was such good friends with Grace..."

"No pressure," Ellen added. "We just didn't know anybody else we could trust. Not who could afford it anyway."

Barbara held the coin up to the light. Quite a little treasure hunt they'd sent her on, looking up each coin. "This 1933 double eagle isn't as old as the others, but it's extremely rare. That's because Roosevelt called for all the gold coins to be melted down before these got circulated. But some still got tucked away by collectors."

The muzak on her line stopped. Barbara sat up. "Yes. I'm still holding." She listened intently. Antique coins weren't so much her specialty, but her old friend gave her all the confirmation she needed. "Definitely," she said. "That inventory I just sent you has verified sale prices I got off the Net for the coins from 1795 through the early 1800s. Then they're more ballpark on the Liberty Heads onward. Most look fine grade to me."

David tugged at Tina's sleeve. "May I see one of her books?"

"Sure," Tina said. "Any one you want. I'm sure it's fine."

Barbara swiveled in her chair. "Seriously, they're barely circulated. Most are practically mint." She gave a thumbs up to the Hollys. "No, no...I'm not looking for a deal here, Morty. I want an honest appraisal for the lot, straight up."

She watched as David selected a volume that probably hadn't left that shelf in decades.

Barbara jotted a note. "Uh-huh... Right, good... Yes, thank you. Nice talking to you again, too." She disconnected and did a quick calculation in her head.

Again, Barbara studied the full array of coins. "It's exquisite, really. Remarkable condition."

His chosen book in hand, David wandered over. "Is it enough to pay off their farm?"

Barbara ran her thumbnail across a lilting grin. "Oh, it's quite a bit more than enough."

LONG AFTER DAVID AND THE HOLLYS had gone, Barbara sat, absently sorting through the collection of gold coins. She'd never been one to buy anything on impulse like that. But somehow, today had been different.

Tina descended a stepladder. "I didn't know you were a coin collector."

"I'm not," Barbara replied. "I just... It's an investment, I guess. No point in having all this money if you don't do something with it, invest it one way or another." She gathered the gold into its sack. "My Aunt Grace, she always talked about investing in people. She invested in me way back and... I think she would have approved of me investing in David. And the Hollys."

Knowing curled on Tina's lips. "Gave 'em even more than it's worth, didn't you?"

A flush heated Barbara's cheeks. She suppressed a smile. Indeed, she had. By far.

"I get that you wanted to do what you did in secret." Tina wiped another shelf. "Just like your aunt used to."

Barbara shrugged. "I guess I wanted to do something, I don't know...large or..." She rose from her desk and gazed out the window. "I've been having this attack of smallness lately. For the past two years actually, since Jack left the city."

Tina scooted over to the next set of shelves. "Can't say I fault a man for tendin' to his own."

"No. I shouldn't." Guilt pressed on Barbara's shoulders. "And I know it's totally unfair of me to hold his relationship with Charlotte against him."

"Miss Somers?" Tina lowered her rag.

"I try to chase those thoughts away, but it's no use. They sneak right back."

"Okay, maybe it's none of my business." Tina stepped closer. "But there's nothing the least bit romantic going on between those two."

Confusion addled Barbara's mind. "There's not? Are you sure?"

"Positive. He just does her legal work. For pay." Compassion shone in Tina's eyes. "Look, I try not to listen to gossip. But small as this town is, if Jack had a thing for anybody, I can tell you, I'd have heard it. Anybody but you, that is."

"Me?" Barbara blinked. "Tina...what makes you think he's interested in me?"

Tina cocked her head. "Not like I claim to know him that well. I don't run in those circles. But I see the other women at church, sniffing 'round Jack Gurnsey, like he was the catch of the day. And can promise you right here and now. He don't look at a one of them the way he looks at you."

The wind left Barbara. For a moment, she could only stand there, her mouth gaping open.

Tina leaned over to pick up her bucket. "Tell you what—if I ever found a man like that—I'd never let him go." With a hike of her brows, she left.

Though Barbara didn't respond, that comment of Tina's hung thick in the air. Smallness reached out its spindly fingers and gripped Barbara all over again.

Despite the extent of her purchase.

In all these years, Tina had never had a chance at a truly good man. Not half the man Barbara had done her best to preemptively reject.

David peered out the window of the town's Savings & Loan office. Outside in the square, some kids gathered around Jack Gurnsey's little sister, Julia. She stroked her kitten, Sally, protectively in her arms.

Behind him, Mr. Streeter bustled through the office door. "Let's get this done. Ain't got all day."

Mr. Holly left Mrs. Holly to come to the window. He leaned to whisper into David's ear. "You sure 'bout this, Son? Miss Holbrook, she'd give the gold back. But once this here is done, it's done."

David nodded. "Daddy said to keep the gold till I need it. And we needed it for this. So, I'm sure."

Mr. Holly patted a warm hand on his back. "All right, then." He headed over to the big desk where the banker man sat.

The banker slid some papers across the desk in the men's direction. "If you'll sign here, Mr. Holly. And you there, Mr. Streeter."

Mr. Holly clicked the pen and signed, then passed the papers to Mr. Streeter. Mrs. Holly glowed like she'd never been so proud.

After blowing the ink, Mr. Holly straightened toward the banker. "An' I want all the rest o' that locked up safe for the boy's schoolin'."

"Of course," the banker said. "We can set that up today, too."

David turned back to the window. Outside, Eugene Streeter sauntered up to Julia. Eugene's friends, Asa and Toby, followed. Julia drew her kitten close. Something in Julia's expression didn't seem so right. David caught Mr. Holly's eye. "Is it okay if I go outside while they finish the papers up?"

"Sure," he said.

"Stay close, Love," Mrs. Holly smiled.

David picked up his violin and started for the door.

As he passed, Mr. Streeter extended a hand to Mr. Holly. "Well, I didn't think you could do it, Holly. But a deal's a deal. Land's yours, now. Free and clear."

As happy as it made David to hear the Hollys had paid off their farm, something tightened in his chest. It hounded him to hurry across the lobby and out the revolving glass door.

BY THE TIME DAVID GOT OUTSIDE and down the steps, a commotion had erupted. Eugene, Asa, and Toby tightened a circle around Julia with three other boys. Where Sally the kitten had gotten to, David couldn't tell.

Julia cowered. "Stop it, Eugene. It's not funny!"

Eugene snorted. "Tie it on her tail, Asa."

"Yeah," Asa hooted. "Take her for a walk."

"Give her back!" Julia lunged toward Eugene.

Eugene tossed Julia toward David like a rag doll. "You're the one that said we could play with your cat."

Finally seeing their game, David gasped in horror. A bag had been tied around Sally the kitten's head.

Asa busied himself, fastening a string to her tail while Toby poked at her with a stick.

David whipped toward Eugene. "Why are you doing that?"

"Oh, lookee." A sneer spread across Eugene's face. "It's the sweet little kitty-lover fiddle boy! Why don't you play a jig for her to dance to?"

Something lit inside David. "Let her go!"

Eugene sauntered threateningly toward David. "You gonna make me, Lover-boy?"

David's mind whirled. There were six of them, older and taller than he. David ducked under Eugene's arm and dashed toward Julia.

Eugene spat on the ground. "Yeah, why don't you two little girls run home, tell your Daddies. Oh, I forgot. Neither of you's got a Daddy, do you?" Eugene snatched up the string on Sally's tail and yanked her around.

Poor little Sally yowled. Blindly, she pawed at her assailants.

Without another thought, David thrust his violin into Julia's arms. He turned back to Eugene, fire blazing within.

Before he knew it, he'd run headlong into the fray. He leapt on top of Eugene with all his might, tackling the boy to the ground. David flailed at Eugene's hand, the one that held the string. Somehow, he had to make Eugene let go.

In a split second, the other five boys jumped David, pulling him off Eugene. Asa landed a punch below David's right eye.

Pain shot through him, but David fought back. He returned Asa's jab, but the other boys pummeled him in a savage flurry. Where he found the fervor, he didn't really know. But fiercely, as he fought those boys, flashes of another long-ago struggle erupted in his memory.

Mama. His angel-mother. Leading him down the city street at age four. A shadowy figure. Accosting her out of nowhere.

David punched furiously at his mother's assailant. His mother struggled valiantly, losing ground.

"Let her go!" little David screamed.

Mama pushed him away. "Run, David! Run!"

Desperately, David still threw himself at her attacker.

In a blur of blows, David rallied back to the present. Fitfully, he slapped at Eugene and his friends.

Julia ran, screaming. "Help! Somebody help him!"

The taste of blood spread on David's tongue, but that didn't stop him from yelling. "Stop it!"

"Stop it!" With all that was in him, young David kicked his mother's attacker.

The boys pulled David off Eugene, yanking back his arms, exposing his midsection.

Eugene, whipped a knife from his pocket. Blindingly, the blade glinted.

That long ago assailant unsheathed his knife, flashing it at little David's mother. "Yeah, you'd better run!"

"Go, David! Run!" Mama cried.

The awful memory flooding back, David hesitated. He stopped flailing at Eugene.

His present attackers took advantage.

Before David knew it, he'd been pinned on his back. Fists flew at his jaw, his stomach, his chest. A sharp, searing pain ripped into his side. David balled up, in agony, but the boys wouldn't relent. They just kept right on pummeling him. Completely without mercy.

"Stop it!" Julia screamed, her fading shouts echoing into the ether. "Stop it, you're killing him!"

But they didn't stop.

Not before everything went black. And the cacophony of voices around David dwindled into absolute silence.

17

Jack Gurnsey boarded the return train to Hinsdale and headed down the aisle. Just ahead of him, Professor Stanton strained to stow her carry-on bag on the railed overhead shelf.

The way she'd dropped everything to go immediately said so much about her. And she'd kept her wits about her, even after Julia called to alert him about what happened to David.

"Let me get that for you." Jack deposited his duffel, then hoisted her bag up to the perch right beside it. Something about that simple act satisfied Jack. Always nice to be able to help someone out, particularly a woman as delightful as this Professor Stanton.

"Would you like the window?" she asked.

"You take it. I had one on the way here." Jack followed her into the row and sat at the aisle beside her.

An older couple eyed the seats facing theirs. "Excuse me," the man said. "Do you mind if we sit across from you and your wife?"

"Please, sit." Jack's temperature rose as he exchanged a glance with Professor Stanton, then turned to the couple. "But we're not married."

A twinkle lit in the man's eye. "But she's your girl, right?"

"No, no," Jack replied. "Actually, we're just traveling together. We've only just met."

"Could have fooled me," the man joked as he and his wife settled in. "Pretty as she is, you might want to consider it."

Professor Stanton's fair complexion reddened.

"Walter, hush." The elderly woman elbowed her hubby. "See now? You're embarrassing her."

"I'm fine." Professor Stanton smiled at the elder gent. "Thank you for the compliment. And I'm sure Mr. Gurnsey will make a fine catch for someone someday." She gave Jack a congenial glance.

Jack averted his attention. What more could he say on the subject without digging this hole any deeper? And yet, silence proved all the more awkward. Traveling with a stranger—and a woman at that—had its challenges.

For the next hour and a half, they'd be side-by-side, moving toward a common destination, yet entirely unfamiliar with each other. All the while, they'd be monitored by those octogenarians, whose hearing seemed unnervingly intact. Should he take out his reader and feign interest in a book? Maybe useless. Not like he could concentrate with David's life in peril.

Somehow Professor Stanton seemed to be holding it together. She leaned his way. "So, you said you used to practice here. I'm curious as to how you decided to leave the city."

"It's complicated." Jack checked the couple across from them. The pair had already occupied themselves with sharing a newspaper. Still, he lowered his voice to a more confidential level. "Kind of a long story. But the short of it is that my adoptive parents died."

Compassion filled her face. "I'm sorry."

"Not easy losing both of them at once."

"I can imagine," she said. "It was kind of like that when I lost my sister, Catherine. Then with my brother-in-law whisking David away like he did—not that I blame him—but it seemed like I'd lost them, too."

"Must have."

Again, silence reigned between them. Finally, she ventured to break it. "Your folks—were they from Hinsdale?"

"Yeah," Jack said. "After I'd left for college, they adopted a baby girl. My younger sister, Julia. So, in addition to being her big brother, when they died I became her legal guardian."

"Wow." She tipped her head. "A child is a lot for a single man to take on."

Jack hiked his shoulders. "Not so much when you love them, like I love her."

"Like I love David," she replied.

Ironic that they had that in common. The tension in Jack's neck eased. Somehow, he could talk to this woman.

Smoothly, the train left the station. Jack checked his watch. Right on time. They could go straight to the hospital. Hopefully, the doctors would be more forthcoming with David's next-of-kin than the others in town. Julia hadn't gleaned much. What they'd be walking into, Jack didn't know. He could only hope to get there in time to be of some help.

Meanwhile, he'd keep a positive attitude with the professor. Best to speak about David in future terms, though no guarantees had been given. "As it happened, leaving the city was pretty much a no-brainer for me. Might be different for you. With all the conservatory could offer to David."

She folded her hands in her lap. "Yes, I've been mulling that over."

"Julia is ten now. And you know, it's just hard to raise a kid alone. Especially in the city. Now more than ever."

"I hear you," she said.

He shook his head. "I don't know how my parent's survived me in my teens. I was, well..."

"A bit of a handful?"

"You could say so." Misadventures flooded Jack's mind. "My two best friends back then—the girl was like an angel on my shoulder. But the guy, Luke, he'd be perched over there on the other extreme. He'd goad me into...well, not the best choices. Stuff that would probably seem tame to kids these days."

"So, who won out with you? The angel or the devil?"

Jack scratched his jaw. "Well, the angel got sent off to boarding school. And let's just say my mom practically wore out her knees praying for me."

"Mine, too."

"Yeah?"

Her nod confirmed it. "Till I was almost seventeen."

"Took much longer for me." The confession stuck in Jack's conscience. "I'm not proud of it, but I suppose it took losing my parents like that to get my attention."

"Must have been tough," she said.

Jack rubbed the emerging stubble on his cheek. "A shame, the way it takes that much sometimes. To make you appreciate what your parents did for you. Now, I'm on my knees about Julia. Same way they were for me."

Professor Stanton hesitated a moment. "Forgive me if this is too personal. But your angel... Is she back there?"

Barbara's face filled Jack's mind. So beautiful, yet so pained. And so distant. "She's there," he said. "But she's not mine. Not anymore."

Simeon Holly wrung his hands as he leaned against the far wall of David's ICU room. Beside him, Ellen wiped another tear. Not a morsel had gone into her mouth since they'd gotten there. But how could he blame her? Not like he could eat either, what with David lying there motionless—that oxygen mask on his battered face. His side stitched and bandaged.

Dr. McBride checked the monitors, whatever all those blips and numbers meant. He lifted David's eyelids, then let them close. No visible reaction from the boy whatsoever. Not in hours.

"Anything?" Simeon searched McBride's face.

"Still breathing pretty well on his own." The doc made a note. "You might as well get some rest."

Simeon planted his feet. "Plenty o' time for rest once that boy's outta the woods." Gratefully, they'd let Ellen and him come into the ICU to stand vigil as David's temporary guardians. Everyone else had crowded into the waiting room, including Perry. The remainder of that corn, it could wait another day, what with David hanging on by a thread.

Last time Simeon checked, looked like most the town had gathered to wait this thing out. Cyrus Higgins followed the ambulance to the hospital. Charlotte Somers alerted everyone on the council who hadn't been in the square to see the trouble. Barbara Holbrook came right away. She'd even given her housekeeper, Tina, time off so she could bring her kids—the blind boy, Joe, and his sister, Betsy. Buck Taylor and Charlie Pepper showed, too.

Seemed like anyone who'd had anything to do with David in the days since he'd arrived had hunkered down in that waiting area. Mollie Tate kept everybody's hopes up. Streeter came after Sheriff Wahl arrested Eugene and his whole band of bullies. Hopefully, that'd put the fear of God into them.

Half an hour later, another nurse came into the ICU and started checking David all over again. Whether that was a good sign or a bad one, who could say? The only thing they told them for sure was that it would take time for David's body to heal from his flesh wounds, and to fight the head trauma.

Ellen stepped toward the nurse. "Any better?"

The nurse shook her head. "No change."

Again, Ellen squeezed her eyes tight and lifted her face up to the ceiling, like she could see straight through it to heaven. "Oh, please. Please, let him wake up."

If this weren't torture Simeon couldn't imagine it. There had to be something else he could do, instead of just waiting there so helpless. Those delinquent boys might have thrown the punches, but Simeon couldn't lay all the blame on them. He pushed off the wall. "Can't just stand here."

WITHIN HALF AN HOUR, Simeon found himself tearing through those woods they'd walked with David, a lantern illuminating his path.

Desperately, Simeon checked the north side of one tree after another. Why hadn't he paid attention to David when they'd gone on that walk? If he had, maybe it wouldn't have been nigh on impossible to find that special moss, the one David told him helped whenever he got sick. "Come on, Moss. Where are you?"

Gasping, Simeon scanned the panorama of trees. So many. And so hard to see now that night had fallen. He slapped at a hungry mosquito. Best keep moving or they'd eat him alive before he could find what he needed.

Why had he let David leave the Savings & Loan in the first place? If he hadn't, David would be safe at home by now. Not beat half to death and in this awful coma.

The distant strains of a virtuoso violinist resonated deep within David's spirit, awakening the innermost part of him. Every stroke of the bow so sweet. So familiar, that crystalline sound.

No one on earth played the violin that way.

No one but Daddy.

Like a faraway dream, the music beckoned, bidding everything in David to leave the past behind and follow.

How had he come to this place? David scanned through the dappled light of a luminous forest. Bright sunbeams streamed through majestic trees. All the while, that melody lilted on the wind.

Daddy.

It must be.

"Daddy, wait..." Despite the aching of his limbs, David broke into a run. A fleeting memory slowed him. Where had his violin gone? Daddy told him in that letter he would expect to see it. Then, just as quickly as the thought occurred, the instrument mysteriously appeared, there in David's hands.

Maybe he could catch up to Daddy, if he hurried. He could go with him. "Daddy...wait."

But just as it seemed David managed to gain ground, Daddy disappeared over the next rise. David pressed his sore frame onward. He gulped for air. "Daddy, wait!"

Breathing came harder and harder, what with his throat so parched. Strange. At their mountain home, he'd skipped up the rocks like a goat. Now, just cresting this hill took every ounce of strength David could muster. Every muscle in his body begged for rest. But he could not stop.

Not now.

Not so close.

He would push through this pain. He had to.

Finally, little farther. And there stood Daddy, walking along their shimmering silver river, toward the horizon. High in the distant light—nearly obscured by its brilliance—moved the silhouetted form of his father. Playing his way step-by-step, toward a glorious city.

The far country.

Dazzlingly, that skyline shone. How beautiful the far country must be. And how wonderful its King. Even their mountain home, in all its splendor, could not compare to the radiance before David. Another cry welled up from within. "Daddy!"

Far ahead, Daddy stopped. Slowly, he turned back in David's direction. Sheer joy emanated from Daddy's face.

"Daddy, wait for me." David called with every fiber of his being. "I'm coming!"

18

Barbara Holbrook shifted in her seat. Many hours had passed since she'd taken up vigil in the ICU waiting room. The sun had long set. And still, not a word of encouragement about David. Not since they'd listed his condition as critical.

Townsfolk camped throughout the area, taking up about every available seat.

Charlotte Somers sat beside Jack's younger sister, quietly reading. In all this time, Charlotte hardly interacted with anyone, let alone Julia. Except for making the unsurprising declaration that she still preferred traditional books to the electronic variety. With that, Charlotte had cracked open a hefty tome. She'd barely spoken a word since.

What was taking Jack so long? He'd been on the distribution list for Charlotte's email. He'd texted to say he'd take the first train home he could and come straight to the hospital.

Barbara thought back. How long had it been since Jack texted her? Years, probably. Since she'd left his last message unanswered and the yawning divide between them had opened.

Betsy Glaspell flipped through channels on the television. So much violence. "Not missing a thing, Joe." Betsy grimaced at her brother. "Nothing on." The twelve year-old tossed the remote atop a stack of dog-eared magazines.

Tina rustled her youngest's hair. "You hungry yet, Joe? Betsy and I can take you to get a bite."

Joe shook his head no. "What if something happens while we're gone?"

Exactly Barbara's worry, when she'd taken the time to visit the hospital's chapel. Odd. With the waiting room bursting at the seams, there hadn't been a soul in the chapel. Even she'd hesitated to stay there very long. But as Aunt Grace always reminded, prayers weren't heard because of their many words, or even where they were offered. And the words Barbara raised had shocked her with their fervency.

Barbara searched her soul. Why she'd gotten so taken up by a child she'd only seen a few times, she couldn't be sure. Never had she met such a boy. The little bow he'd taken as he'd dubbed her his Lady of the Roses brought an affectionate rise to her lips.

His affinity for nature and music and books. The way he'd read the Latin phrase on her sundial. And mostly, how he'd seen through her reserved exterior to that pervasive melancholy she suffered.

Regret twisted in Barbara. Why hadn't she shown David to his father's grave yet? It hadn't seemed the time when he'd been over about the gold with the Hollys. She'd made that note to send for him later. And now... Well, later might not come to be. Not with David's condition so grave. Quietly, she closed her eyes.

Please. Save him.

For a moment, peace flooded Barbara. Until she opened her eyes again and saw Jack, rushing into the waiting area, a winsome woman at his side.

Simeon removed David's oxygen mask. "He's still breathin' okay." That's when it hit him. As long as it had taken to find that moss, then to hurriedly make the tea, he hadn't thought things through. With David in a coma, how in the blessed world could he get the boy to drink the concoction?

Those moans Ellen let out every other second didn't help. Neither did the ruts she kept pacing in the ICU's floor.

He withdrew the cup and stepped back as a nurse passed in the hall. After coming this far, it'd be plain terrible if some do-gooder tried to stop him in the name of by-the-book red tape.

When the coast seemed clear, Simeon put the cup to David's mouth. "Come on. Drink, Boy."

"Simeon, I don't think he can swallow. He might choke on it. Or it could be the wrong moss. What if it's poison? You can't just—"

"Hush now, Ellen. Let me try. Trust if it ain't s'posed to go down, it won't." He pressed the cup against David's lips, but for what? Most of the tea spilled uselessly down those battered cheeks.

Simeon set the cup aside and blotted the wetness away. "Just like everything else. I can't do nothin'." He covered his face with his palms.

Ellen stroked his slumped shoulders. "That's not true, Simeon. You can put him in hands bigger than yours. You can pray."

Once in a while, the woman had a point. Right then and there, Simeon bowed to his knees.

A murmur interrupted his plea—so soft he almost didn't hear it. Then again, there it came.

From David.

Scratchily, the whisper sounded. "Daddy..." The boy winced.

Ellen's hands flew to her heart. "Sweet Jesus, thank you."

In a flash, Simeon went to his bedside. "David?" He scooped the boy's hand into his.

Another half-conscious mumble came from David as his lids fluttered open. "Daddy..."

The lump that rose in Simeon's throat just about choked him. And the tears, there'd be no stopping them. "I'm here, Son," he said. "I'm here."

Jack signaled Professor Stanton to wait in the hall, then entered David's ICU room. Though David's wounds would take time to heal, the crisis had passed. With David sitting up, sipping a curious-looking cup of tea, it seemed he'd turned a corner. "David?"

"You're that lawyer," David replied. "Is Julia's kitten okay?"

"Yes." Jack marveled at the irony. "As a matter of fact, she is. And my sister sends you her thanks."

Simeon and Ellen Holly stepped back.

"David," Jack said. "I told you I'd be checking some things out for you. Well, I've been to the city and...there's someone here who..." He headed back toward the door. "Someone I brought with me. She'd like very much to see you."

Simeon drummed his arm. "You sure this is okay? They've been saying no visitors, not 'cept family."

Jack smiled. "It's okay." He leaned out the doorway and beckoned Professor Stanton. "Come on in."

He stayed back as the professor entered. Still, Jack couldn't miss the hint of recognition that registered in David's eyes.

"Wait..." David peered into Professor Stanton's face. He glanced at his violin case, now in her hand.

Her complexion aglow, she crossed to David's bed. She stood there beside him like not a moment had passed in the six years that had separated them. Serenely, she held his gaze.

"Who are you?" David asked. "Do I..."

Jack looked on as Professor Stanton reached into her pocket, and then perched on the edge of the bed beside David. She unfolded the photocopies Jack had made, the letters from her brother-in-law, David's father. Quietly, she extended the papers.

A mystified calm came over David. "How did you get Daddy's letters?"

Professor Stanton's eyes welled as she looked into David's battered face. "I'm sorry. It's just so..." She lowered her gaze and pressed a finger to her lips, clearly doing her best to contain her brimming tears. Collecting herself, she showed David a passage of the letter. "This part your father wrote...where he tells you '*Hope awaits you in the world...*' That's my name there. I'm your Aunt Hope, David. That's me."

SCARCELY A MOMENT PASSED BEFORE JACK felt a tug on his arm and Simeon Holly escorted him into the hallway. For a man who'd just gotten exactly what he wanted, Simeon sure looked conflicted. Whereas the man had been positively bent upon getting David out of his house, now the tide seemed to have turned.

Simeon set his voice at a low, but urgent level. He pointed an index finger insistently. "I ain't givin' the boy up. That's all there is to it."

"I understand," Jack said. "But you have to consider the legalities here. Professor Stanton, she's family. She wants him."

"An' I don't?" Simeon said. "We was there for him, Gurnsey."

"I know you were." Jack measured his words. "But she's a relative. She has rights."

Simeon backpedaled toward the room. "Yeah, well... So do the boy."

Jack rubbed at his jaw. This would be harder than it seemed. No question what the law required, but Simeon Holly wouldn't take this sitting down. Not the way he'd just reacted. And the last thing David needed would to be stuck in some kind of protracted legal conflict, with people who were supposed to want the best for him, tearing him apart.

Jack untangled his thoughts as he headed for the waiting room. This could get sticky and fast. And if Jack didn't want half the town to weigh in on this thing, he'd best get them out of there. He'd give them the good news they'd been waiting for, that David had regained consciousness. He'd stick to the basics about who David and his father were, then send them all home for the night.

Even Barbara.

Despite the way her eyes implored him for more. As much as Jack longed to share all the details of his trip with Barbara personally, that would have to wait.

BY THE TIME JACK RETURNED to David's room, the tension had dissipated a bit. But the determined set of Simeon Holly's jaw spoke loud and clear. Jack hadn't heard the last of this. Simeon wouldn't make a scene now. Not in front of the boy. But he wouldn't let this go. Not by a long shot.

It appeared that David hadn't picked up on the conflict. He'd sat himself up, more erect than before. Ellen and Hope flanked him on either side, chatting like best friends.

David's eyes widened at Hope. "Do you mean Daddy was famous?"

Hope smiled warmly. "He was what they call a virtuoso." She patted the case she'd set on the table. "Your violin...It's a very special one. It's a child's size. Made by a master violinmaker by the name of Amati."

"Yes," David said. "Daddy told me."

Simeon's brow knitted. "Wait. You saying that old thing's worth somethin'?"

Ellen nudged her husband's arm. "Simeon!"

David set an affectionate gaze on the case. "It's worth the world to me."

Hope stroked David's arm. "And that will always be its greatest value." She looked back at the Hollys. "But yes, Mr. Holly. It's worth quite a bit. Not as much as it would have been if the bridge hadn't been replaced." She turned back to David, her eyes shining. "But your father's violin—that one... I'll never forget the sound when he played. It's a Stradivarius."

Jack rocked back. "Probably worth a fortune."

Simeon's jaw dropped. "That bucket o' scraps you loaned out to that blind kid, Joe Glaspell?"

Hope took David's hand. "Your daddy played that violin on stages all over the world."

Ellen smiled at David. "So, maybe you weren't just dreamin' of that orchestra you told Perry about after all."

David lit up. "That was real?"

Hope nodded, a bittersweet look tempering her joy. She shot a questioning look toward Jack. Almost to ask if telling David now would be too much too soon.

"I think it's okay," Jack assured. "He's old enough to know."

Hope turned back to David, her eyes freshly gleaming. "Your father... You, your mother and I, we went to hear him with the Philharmonic. It was the last night I saw you."

David gazed back at his aunt. "You were there?"

"Yes, David." She spoke so quietly, almost reverently. "I was."

19

Tina Glaspell tucked her kids under their covers. First Betsy, then Joe. Never had she let them stay up anywhere near so late. But neither of them would have slept a wink anyway. Not till they heard that David was out of danger.

Good thing they could sleep in tomorrow. So nice of Barbara to give her the morning off—and with pay at that. Barbara probably needed the rest as much as they did.

A furious pounding erupted at her front door. Tina's heart sank.

"Tina! I know you're home."

She groaned. Luke. Drunk again, from that slur in his voice.

"Open up, Tina." He punctuated the shout with a flurry of slaps against the siding.

Betsy rolled over. "Make him go away, Mama."

Tina turned off their light. "Trust me. I will."

She ground her teeth as she made her way out toward the front door. What a vicious cycle. Absolute crazy-making. How many times had she begged God to take Luke out of her life? And still, there he stood, banging on her door, caterwauling to high heaven.

"Tina, come on!"

She set the safety chain in place, then cracked the door ajar.

"What's with the chain?" he said. "Lemme in."

"No, Luke."

"No? What makes you think you can say no to me?" He smashed his beer bottle against the door. Shards of brown glass scattered. "You let me in this second or I swear to you, I'm breakin' this door down."

Inside, Tina trembled. But she couldn't let him see that. "Leave, Luke. Or I'm callin' Sheriff Wahl."

Fire lit in Luke's eyes. In a flash, he raised his foot and kicked the door, so hard it broke the chain and sent Tina reeling.

Luke thrashed around the living room, tearing the place apart.

"Stop it, Luke!"

"Where is it?" Spit flew with his snarls. "You're such a poser, Tina. Cryin' poor all the time. Thing's probably worth millions."

Tina scrambled up to her feet, just as Betsy and Joe appeared from the hall, their faces gripped with terror.

"Leave her be!" Betsy cried.

As Luke spewed his venom, Joe felt his way to behind the chair at the window. He grabbed the violin case and cradled it to his chest.

Tina threw herself between Luke and her son. "Get out!"

Luke charged at her. "Give it to me!"

"Leave, Luke!" She jabbed a point to the door.

With a glare, he grabbed her wrist. Tossing her aside, he swung back toward Joe.

Betsy wailed hysterically.

Again, Tina rose. "Betsy, call Sheriff Wahl. Do it, now." She clawed at Luke's back, but in an instant, he whirled. Pain shot through her cheek as he slapped her away.

Luke ripped the violin case from Joe as Betsy ran for the phone.

"You can't have it!" Joe flailed blindly at Luke. "It ain't mine!"

Holding the case out of the boy's reach, Luke scoffed. "You gonna take me on, Boy?"

With everything she could rally, Tina thrashed at Luke. "Get away from him! In the holy name of Jesus, leave us alone."

Luke spun back at her, his face contorted—like the man she'd once known wasn't there anymore. He staggered toward the door with the violin. "Yeah, I'm leavin' all right. I'm gone!"

Simeon Holly pulled on his jacket. Most had cleared out of the hospital waiting room, but Sheriff Wahl, Streeter, and Perry had hung out to hear Jack's explanation to this whole outlandish story.

Simeon scratched his noggin. "This don't make no sense, Jack. Why's a world famous violinist gonna up and leave it all? To go raise his son like a hermit on a mountain? Not even tell him his whole name?"

"Because of what he saw," Jack said. "Who he saw."

Perry shook his head.

The sheriff narrowed his gaze. "Ever get the guy?"

"Never did. Cold case." Jack pulled his car keys out. "The only suspect didn't check out with DNA evidence. With them being in the limelight the way they were—and his son as the only eyewitness—

David's father took off with him. He just couldn't risk it."

"Lot to give up," Streeter said.

Jack shrugged. "Depends on how you look at it, I guess." He set eyes on Simeon.

Simeon averted his gaze. Seemed like David's Daddy had completely given up the farm. So to speak, that is. He'd walked away from fame and fortune overnight. All to protect that young boy of his. An unsettling truth rested in Simeon's stomach. Couldn't fault a man who'd set his own desires aside, all for that particular child.

SIMEON HARDLY SAID A WORD while Ellen tucked David into bed. The hospital had washed him up good before sending him home with them. But the cuts, scrapes, and bruises from the attack, they'd be awhile mending.

Dullness swept over David's face. Gone was the life that had been in his eyes, ever since he showed up in their barn.

Ellen brushed his hair back. "What is it, Love?"

The boy's eyes glistened. A moment passed before he spoke. "My angel-mother... That man sent her to the far country on purpose, didn't he?"

Ellen traded a look with Simeon, as if asking how much to say. "You remember?"

"I think so," David said. "The dream, it was real, wasn't it?"

Ellen quieted David with a pat of his hand. "Let's not think about that now. We promised Dr. McBride you'd sleep. Your Aunt Hope, she'll be over to check on you later in the day. And I told her I'd make sure you rested." Ellen squeezed his arm, then headed out.

Simeon lingered. "I'll be along."

Ellen pulled the door to as she left. Her way of hinting that he should stay. Till he said what she thought he ought.

He pulled up a wooden chair and sat down by David.

The boy looked mighty conflicted. "Aunt Hope says I'm to go with her, that she teaches at a school where I can study."

"That she does," Simeon nodded.

His blue eyes darkened. "Daddy always told me the world was beautiful."

"Mm-hmm."

Absently, David stared away. "Seems like there may be some things in the world Daddy didn't know about."

"What do you mean, Boy?"

A tear rolled down David's battered cheek. "Like about what happened to my angel-mother. I remember, now. And it's so ugly."

Simeon hung his head. "Can't argue with you about that."

David set his hand on Simeon's. "I don't want to go into the world. Not if it's like that. Not if..." His voice broke. "I want to stay here on the farm with you and Mrs. Holly and Perry Larson and—"

"Hush, now." Simeon steeled himself. But knowing what he had to do didn't make it one bit easier. "Course you'll go. An' it's not that I'm wantin' you to leave. Truth is, I want you here. I'm not sure when it was you wiggled your way into my heart, but you did. And I do love you, Son. More 'n I can rightly say."

Something in David's gloom lifted. A soft smile curved.

Simeon glanced out the window, toward his cornfields, lit by the rising run. "Tell you what, David. That dirt on this land was uglier 'n sin thirty years ago. But my daddy told me, just like yours told you in that letter...ugly don't always have to be that way."

"No?"

"Naw," Simeon said. "You just get out there with your dirt or whatever it is. Whatever field the good Lord gives you to plant. You work that land hard. Next thing you know something real pretty is comin' up."

Fear fleeted across David's face. "But what about that man? That man who... I saw him."

"Don't you worry yourself another second about him." He patted David's hand. "Prob'ly long gone or locked up for somethin' else. Been most o' six years, now."

"No," David insisted. "No, he's not gone. I saw him. Here, in town."

Jack lingered in the shadows of the train station with Sheriff Wahl. Providentially, he'd still been going over what he'd learned with the sheriff when the call from the Glaspells came in, alerting them that Luke had taken off with the Stradivarius.

For once, Luke's inebriated state seemed an advantage. That stupor would slow the guy down and blur his thinking about getting away. Luke's car had been repossessed long ago, so it didn't take much to figure he'd try to skip town by rail.

Growing up, running with Luke in his teens, Jack hadn't seen it coming to this. But then again, the writing had been on the wall.

For ages.

When Luke got sober a while back, the affable side of him gave Jack hope. But Luke and the wagon parted ways repeatedly. And alcohol brought out the worst. Still, Jack could hardly imagine that a guy he'd once called a friend had fallen so far.

Sheriff Wahl tapped Jack. He set a silencing finger to his mouth, then pointed down the block where Luke stumbled toward the station.

Jack prepared himself. This would be it. Luke would turn on him, even more fiercely than he already had. He'd call him a traitor for standing on the law's side. Jack slumped. He took no pleasure in this. But bringing Luke to justice might be just the shock Luke needed. If this didn't turn the guy around, nothing would.

Luke stepped up to the ticket booth. He set a large duffel bag down at his feet and slapped some cash on the counter. "Put me on the next train."

"Where you headed?" the clerk asked.

"Whatever," Luke replied. "I don't care where."

As soon as the clerk took Luke's money, Sheriff Wahl drew his weapon. He signaled Jack to make his approach.

Jack ambled over toward the ticket window as Sheriff Wahl moved into position, cornering Luke between the station walls.

He fought to calm his pounding pulse. Their moment of truth had come.

Luke took his receipt. He glanced at the ticket, then picked up the duffel.

"So, Luke..." Jack said.

Luke whirled.

Nonchalantly, Jack hiked his brows. "Whatcha got in the bag?"

THE NEXT DAY COULDN'T COME SOON ENOUGH. Not as far as Jack was concerned. But David needed rest and recovery, before they could bring him down to the jail.

Practically every man David had met there came forward to stand in the lineup, though most had done nothing wrong. The pastor appeared first, then Charlie Pepper, Dr. McBride, and the church organist took their places. Luke Dowd came out in the fifth position. Cyrus Higgins and Bill Streeter brought up the rear.

From the safety of the next room, David watched through an observation window.

Sheriff Wahl punched the intercom to speak to the men. "All right, face forward everybody. Hold your number over your chest."

Jack set a reassuring hand on David's shoulder. "He can't see you."

David looked up at Jack, a pained expression in his eyes. "But I can see him." Clearly petrified, David opened his hand to gaze once more at the small, framed photo of his angel-mother. Then squarely, he looked up at Luke. "Number five."

Jack exchanged a look with Sheriff Wahl, then turned back to David. "Are you sure you remember, David? I know it was a long time ago and you were only four. Are you positive that's the man you saw in the city...the one who attacked your mother?"

David nodded forlornly, his eyes filling.

JACK LOOKED ON AS SHERIFF WAHL escorted Luke to a holding cell and clanged the door shut. Apparently, the alcohol had begun to leave Luke's system. But his propensity toward rage hadn't.

Luke spat through the bars. "You can't do this!"

Sheriff Wahl lifted a key. "Turn your back and raise your hands to me. Unless you want to stay cuffed in there."

Snarling, Luke swung around. As soon as the sheriff reached through and extracted the restraints, Luke spun, spittle spraying. "I'm suin' all of you, I am. Every lousy one of you! Ain't no judge listenin' to no bogus ID from some stupid kid." He shot an expectant look at Jack. "Tell him, Jack."

Jack watched the sheriff carefully preserve Luke's sample-splattered shackles. "You forget, we have DNA from the killer. Something tells me yours will be a match." Steadily, Jack held Luke's gaze. "I'd suggest you get yourself another lawyer, Luke. I'll be with the prosecution." Determinedly, he turned to follow Sheriff Wahl away.

Luke rattled his cage, yelling after him. "You got nothin' on me! Absolutely nothin'. You ain't no lawyer, Gurnsey! You're a failure. A babysitter for cryin' out loud. You're just a worthless, washed up wad of nothin'!"

His spine straight, Jack kept pace down the hall. Never once did he look back. The accusations Luke hurled faded into the distance. There'd been a time when Jack would have let those knives sink into his spirit, but no longer. This time, they clattered harmlessly to the ground. Instead of listening to the voice of his accuser, he listened to the voice of God.

And that made all the difference.

20

Barbara Holbrook peeked through the sheers of her bedroom window, overlooking Sunnycrest's circular drive. They'd be there any minute. Jack had always been the punctual sort. Dependable to a fault.

He'd gladly taken care of extending Barbara's invitation to visit the grave on her property. And he'd been completely accommodating about driving. Though Jack lived just across the creek, he'd offered to run over to the Hollys' farm to pick up David, then to drop by the town's Bed & Breakfast to give David's Aunt Hope a lift.

Barbara glanced in the full-length mirror. Had it been a mistake to put on that dress? Would it be interpreted as a show of respect, or as a thinly veiled attempt to compete with Hope and recapture Jack's eye? One of these days, she'd have to stop over-thinking everything, every last detail having to do with Jack Gurnsey.

Right on the button, Jack's sedan turned down the lane into Sunnycrest's circular drive. He motored to a stop down front. Quickly, he popped out and rounded the sedan, then opened the passenger doors—first Hope's, then David's.

Ever the gentleman. Or perhaps Jack intended to impress the attractive professor. They'd seemed so familiar at the hospital, then sitting together at church, flanking their respective ten-year-olds. Already, Jack and Hope had so much in common.

Barbara banished the thought. If she were too late for Jack, she had no one to blame but herself. She started down the staircase just as Tina answered the door. As they entered, looking every bit like a family in the making, Barbara's attempt at a smile quivered. The rail steadied her steps, but did nothing for her breaking heart.

She sent up a silent plea for strength. The answer saturated through her, like a cup of cold water on a hot summer's day. Barbara squared her shoulders and set a pleasant expression in place. Somehow, she'd get through this.

FROM A RESPECTFUL DISTANCE, Barbara watched Jack as he stood with Hope and David at the graveside.

The man in her plot had more than a name now. To David, he'd always be Daddy, and to Hope, her brother-in-law. But with Jack's cracking of that long cold case, and the resulting media coverage, the world now knew who'd been buried in the Holbrook private cemetery.

So curious, to think that Barbara stood last in that distinguished line of Holbrooks. One day she, too, would be laid to rest there. By whose hands, she couldn't imagine.

Only that it wouldn't be family.

Compassion filled Barbara as she noted David's face, his exposed lower arms. Those terrible bruises had begun to fade and his abrasions had started to heal. Unthinkable, what those boys had done to that precious child. Let alone Julia's kitten. Why must the innocent suffer so?

Barbara's eyes drifted to Aunt Grace's plot and the epitaph on her grave marker:

Beloved Aunt, Child of God.

Aunt Grace had only asked for that last part. But the initial descriptor Barbara added brought a measure of comfort. How dearly she adored Aunt Grace. Still. Death hadn't touched that, any more than it could ever separate David from his father. Through eternity, some things never changed. Some people survived the greatest fires of this life without even the hint of smoke. And those lasting sacrifices of love they'd made bound them together forever.

Like scales falling off, Barbara saw Hope with new eyes. David would come to love and treasure his aunt. Hope would mean just as much to the boy as Aunt Grace had meant to her. And if that meant Barbara would lose Jack, then so be it. This boy deserved someone to cherish him, the way Hope Stanton surely would.

Hope wrapped an arm around David. Together, they stood at the mound of earth covering his father's grave.

David raised those azure eyes toward Jack. "This is where?"

Jack nodded. "You okay?"

Peacefully, the boy's chest rose and fell, almost with a hint of detachment. "It's only what he left behind. He's in the far country. With my angel-mother."

Hope combed her fingers through the top of David's hair. "That's right, Sweetheart. And we'll always think of them there. You know, the gospels say that's what heaven is like. Like a man who went to a far country."

David smiled. He leaned over with a small brass plate. Lovingly, he placed it over his father's grave, then peered toward Jack for approval.

Jack tipped his head, looking every bit the proud uncle. "A good name for a good man."

Another attack of smallness pressed at Barbara. Her motives for burying the man there hadn't been altogether pure at first. But given what she now knew, gratitude rose in her spirit. Not to have a famous violinist in her plot. That she'd stumbled into. But how wonderful to have had that place for a man so deeply loved by his kin.

"Now, what should we do?" David asked.

Hope drew David close. "We follow his example. No matter what else. You know, David... Something terrible, something truly ugly happened in his life. There's no denying that. But still...somehow, he found a greater purpose for living. A way to move on in the world."

David's face became quietly resplendent. "He made it beautiful."

"Yes," Jack said. "That he did."

In time, Hope wandered to Barbara's side. She gestured over her shoulder, back toward Jack and David. "Nice for David to have a man like Jack in his life. Given everything that's happened."

"It is." Barbara dabbed her cheeks with a tissue. "And he is a good man. Jack, I mean."

Wonderment seemed to envelop Hope. "And to think, if Jack hadn't come to the city, if he hadn't done what he did. If he hadn't found me... Well, we wouldn't be here. Would we?"

Barbara wrestled within. Somewhere, she had to find the selflessness she lacked. The courage to confirm that last nagging assumption. If nothing else, it would give her closure. "Will Jack be accompanying you and David, back to the city?"

"Jack says he..." Hope searched Barbara's eyes, as if she could see right through them, all the way to her fear. "He'll be commuting back and forth during the day, once school starts up for Julia. Working again...it seems it's been good for him."

"Yes." Barbara averted her gaze. "So it seems." Obviously, she'd been right in what she'd intuited. Any chance she'd had with Jack had slipped through her fingers for good.

Hope directed Barbara toward Jack. "You know that Jack, he..." Softly, Hope set a hand on Barbara's arm. "He is so very much in love with you."

"But I thought..." Stunned, Barbara looked at Jack, then turned back to Hope. "Did he say so?"

"Not in so many words," Hope replied. "But a woman knows these things."

David raised his violin, as if inspiration had wafted by on a breeze. A sweetly mournful melody told the tale of the life they'd come to honor. As David poured out his heart through those strings, a soaring crescendo rose. It sang of a future that lay beyond the grave, in that far country each of them would one day come to call home.

THAT NIGHT, A SECOND VIOLIN joined David's as most of the town gathered at the Hollys' farm for a two-fold celebration. With festive lanterns hung about, the evening had been dubbed a part mortgage burning and part fond farewell party.

Jack had been the one to email the invitation to Barbara at Simeon Holly's request. Tina had received one for herself and the kids, too. And a look at Tina in that new dress she'd bought her made Barbara glad she'd insisted.

As Betsy led Joe along by the hand, Barbara whispered into Tina's ear. "Remember, you're not working this party tonight. You're a guest."

Tina scanned the size of the gathering. "Lots of people here. What would I even say to anybody? Besides. Who's going to watch my kids?"

Barbara guided Tina into the throng around David and Hope. "They'll be fine. Just go on. Have a good time."

"I don't know," Tina replied. "Hardly know what to do with myself if I'm not helping." She reached to take a casserole from Charlotte Somers. "Let me get that for you, Miss Somers."

"Oh," Charlotte said. "Thank you."

Off Tina's cue, Barbara relieved Charlie Pepper of an enormous pasta salad. "This looks delicious."

Proudly, Charlie took his wife's hand. "Sarah's specialty. She did the hard part. I just carried the bowl."

As the Peppers coaxed their brood on, Barbara spotted Jack. She wouldn't seek him out. Not yet. Instead, she and Tina stationed themselves to spread out potluck goodies from arriving guests. Soon, the service tables could barely hold the bounty.

For an hour or more they feasted together as a community, under the starlit night. They circulated around, catching up about every little thing. Letting one another into their hearts. Like neighbors are supposed to do.

After everyone had their fill, Jack's voice rang out. "Come on, folks. Gather 'round." He motioned toward the steps leading up to the Hollys' house.

Atop their porch, Simeon Holly lit a ceremonial match, then gave his wife a signal. Ellen pulled out a copy of the farmland's paid-off mortgage. With a flourish, she set the edge aflame, then plunked it into a metal waste basket to burn. Bill Streeter let out a hoot, cheering along with the rest of them.

Music erupted. With David on the Amati and his Aunt Hope on the Stradivarius, the valley resounded with an uncommonly infectious tune. Men, women, and children alike ran to dance to the lively duet.

Contentment filled Barbara as she scanned across the yard at the people of Hinsdale. What a good time Jack seemed to be having. Freely, he kicked up his heels with his little sister, Julia, to the girl's obvious delight. Buck Taylor grabbed Mollie Tate and pulled her into a dance, too. Charlie Pepper set spoons together and pounded out a rhythm on his thigh. Young Joe Glaspell clapped in time. Soon half the crowd had paired up to dance to the music.

Barbara's breath caught as Perry Larson made his way toward Tina. Respectfully, the farmhand tipped his cap. "I'm real sorry, Tina. Hearin' about Luke an' all."

Shyly, Tina shrugged. "It's for the best, I guess. Anyway, I'm trusting that it will be."

Barbara watched Perry. The guy never wavered as he held Tina's gaze. "Fine woman like you. Two growin' kids... You deserve a good man."

Behind them, David and Hope transitioned the tune into a welcoming ballad.

Perry motioned toward the others. "Sounds like a slow one." He extended his hand to Tina.

Tina traded a happy glance with Barbara, then placed her hand in Perry's. "That's okay," Tina said. "I like to take things slow."

A kind of awe came over Barbara as she watched Perry lead Tina toward the dancers, then take the single mother into his arms. Sometimes you just knew when something wonderful had begun. Deep down.

And this had to be one of those times.

"Excuse me." Ellen Holly tapped Barbara's shoulder. "I have something for Joe." She held out a well-worn violin. "It's my son's student model. If that's okay."

Barbara cleared a path toward Joe. "I'm sure his mother will appreciate that."

Ellen leaned down to Joe and extended the violin. "It's not so fine as the other one, the one you returned to David."

Barbara drank in the rapture on Joe Glaspell's face as he examined John Holly's instrument with his fingertips.

"It was John's." Affection shone in Ellen's eyes. "My son's. And I'd like you to have it, Joe."

Joe trained his blind eyes toward the sound of Ellen's voice. "For keeps?"

"Yes, Joe. For keeps." Ellen ran her hand across the instrument one last time. "David tells me that a violin, it wants to be played. Will you do that for me, Joe?"

A radiant smile stretched across Joe's face. "I promise. I will."

Simeon moseyed over and set an arm around Ellen. Barbara watched as Simeon looked across the throng of their friends and neighbors. "Not much more a man can ask for out o' life. Not much more than this."

Ellen nodded sweetly, but Barbara couldn't miss the faraway look in the woman's eyes. With a fond pat on her husband's tummy, Ellen headed toward the house. "I suppose I should check on things in the kitchen."

Barbara gazed across the crowd. Where had Jack gotten to? Ah, there. Trading bows with his sister, Julia. Apparently, they'd skip the slow dance. Something seemed so different about Jack's bearing. Confidence, maybe. A new contentment.

She turned toward Betsy. "You'll look after Joe for awhile, won't you?"

"Sure," Betsy said.

Almost without thinking, Barbara found herself making her way toward Jack. A prayer resonated within. *Please, let Hope be right.* Could it really be that Jack longed for Barbara just as deeply as she longed for him?

He turned at her light tap on his shoulder. "Oh. Ms. Holbrook..."

Steadily, Barbara held his gaze. There would be no childish hints, no stilted formalities, no mixed signals. Not this time. "Dance with me, Jack."

Delight sparkled in Jack's eyes as he took her hand in his and spun her so gracefully, into his welcoming arms.

Barbara reveled in the newness of his touch. How many years had she waited for this kind of nearness? Not with just anyone. With him. Such a long time in coming. And yet, in the magnificence of the moment, it seemed no time had passed.

Ever so tenderly, Jack whispered into her ear. "You remember how much we meant to each other?"

Barbara's eyes glistened as she swayed in the warmth of his embrace. "I do."

"I want us to be friends again," he whispered. "That and so much more."

She savored every second. Those words she'd ached to hear. The effervescence that tingled all through her, just to be there in Jack's embrace.

For a while, she could scarcely breathe, much less open her eyes. But when she did, beyond them, she caught a glimpse of David and his Aunt Hope. They continued to play, all smiles in her direction.

Jack nuzzled against Barbara's cheek, then brushed it with a kiss. Not a neighborly peck. Not a brotherly show of affection.

A real kiss. Brimming with promise.

That simple act said everything Barbara's heart needed to hear. This was no flight of fancy. No sudden whim. Jack saw her the way she'd only dreamed. Not as some make-believe princess in a tower. As a real, grown woman. One he'd chosen.

For life.

Music from the ongoing party wafted through the open windows of the Hollys' farmhouse. Slyly, Simeon peered into the kitchen. With half the town enjoying themselves in the yard, there Ellen stood, puttering around at the sink. That long-suffering woman who'd put up with his nonsense for thirty-some years. She'd stood like a rock at his side. Even after he'd blown it so sky high with John.

Funny. After all those eons slaving to pay off that farm—and as happy as Ellen had seemed to burn the note—that trace of wistfulness still hung in her amber eyes. Not much he could do about that now.

Or could he?

Before he could put it off any longer, Simeon snatched up the kitchen phone. He pointed to the faded number Ellen had scribbled ages ago, attached to the refrigerator with a magnet. That number he'd never once dialed, not since all the trouble between them.

"This number still good for John?" He began to punch the digits in.

Ellen turned, her eyes searching his. "Yes... Simeon, are you—"

He waved her down. "Hush, Woman. It's ringing already."

She came to his side and wrapped her arms around him. Like he'd just bought her a diamond as big as their barn.

That familiar voice sounded through the other end of the receiver. "Hello?"

"Uh, hello...Son, this is—" He traded a wry glance with Ellen. "It's your Mom and Dad."

Ellen looked up with such adoration, like that ever lovin' heart of hers might bust right to pieces.

With his spare arm, Simeon snuggled his wife's middle. "Well, it's been a long while and... Yes, Son, it's mighty good to hear your voice, too."

SIMEON COUNTED HEADS ON THE train platform. Seemed like the folks of Hinsdale couldn't get enough of one another. Most everybody who'd come to the party showed up at the station to see David off that next morning. Hard to believe the time had come to say goodbye to the little fella.

Jack Gurnsey shook David's hand with a nod toward the horizon. "Make it beautiful, David."

David returned a smile. "I will."

No sooner than Jack retrieved his hand from David's, he slipped it around Barbara Holbrook's back. Simeon snickered as he leaned close to Ellen's ear. "Those two sure have gotten cozy. Ever since last night."

Ellen grinned. "Just the way her Aunt Grace always hoped and prayed."

"Seems Perry has taken up with the Glaspell woman, too." Simeon motioned in Tina's direction. "Not that I'd have called it. But ain't a bad match. Perry needs somebody. Like I need you."

When Barbara offered her hand to David, the boy bent down to kiss it. "Goodbye, my Lady of the Roses."

Whatever that had to do with anything, Simeon couldn't say, but Barbara accepted it right off. "*Horas non numero nisi serenas*," Barbara said to David.

Just more gibberish to Simeon. "Say what?"

Almost at once, Barbara and David translated, "Count none but sunny hours."

Ellen circled David in a bear hug, then handed him a big box of candy she'd wrapped up special. "Chocolate. For your trip."

That got a beam outta the boy. Just like Ellen said it would.

But that smile on David's face faded when he looked up at Simeon's. Those blue eyes pooled. "How can I say goodbye to you?"

Simeon sniffed back a tear of his own as he lifted David's quivering chin. "You don't, Son. You just get on that train there an' you go find that work your Daddy told you that you gotta do in the world. You promise me?"

"I promise," David replied.

Simeon wrapped his arms around David. The boy held on tight for the longest time, squeezing the stuffing right outta him. No telling how long they might have stayed there, if Simeon hadn't pulled away. "Run along, now. Or you'll miss your train. And remember, we'll be up to visit 'fore you blink."

Hope rested a hand on David's shoulder. "You ready, Sweetheart?"

Simeon sighed. Hard to know if he'd ever be ready to see the boy go, but it did seem right. Like things went the way somebody bigger than him must've had it planned. Like something more than corn had grown for him this season.

David followed his Aunt Hope to the train. They shot up a final wave to the crowd.

That platform teemed with every life David had touched, not the least Simeon's own. Everyone called out their goodbyes. Julia Gurnsey flagged her kitten's paw. The women blew their kisses. Jack and Barbara waved, hand in hand. Perry, Tina, and her kids, too.

As David stepped through the door to the train car, Ellen slipped an arm around Simeon. "We'll be up to visit soon, you say?"

Simeon nodded, his gaze fixed on the train. "In a few weeks. When I'm takin' us to see John." No missing Ellen's bliss over hearing those words, that promise he'd made to God and himself. A promise he'd surely keep.

Soon, David appeared at a window. As the train departed the station, the boy raised his violin. Once more, he began to play. The melody grew fainter as the train pulled away. But Simeon looked on—a new man—David's song still ringing in his ears.

About the Author of The Beautiful World

SUSAN ROHRER is an honor graduate of James Madison University where she studied Art and Communications, and thereafter married in her native state of Virginia.

A professional writer, producer, and director specializing in redemptive entertainment, Rohrer's credits in one or more of these capacities include: a screen adaptation of *God's Trombones;* 100 episodes of drama series *Another Life;* Humanitas Prize finalist & Emmy winner *Never Say Goodbye;* Emmy nominees *Terrible Things My Mother Told Me* as well as *The Emancipation of Lizzie Stern;* anthology *No Earthly Reason;* NAACP Image Award nominee *Mother's Day;*

AWRT Public Service Award winner (for addressing the problem of teen sexual harassment) *Sexual Considerations;* comedy series *Sweet Valley High;* telefilms *Book of Days,* and *Another Pretty Face;* Emmy nominee & Humanitas Prize finalist *If I Die Before I Wake;* as well as Film Advisory Board & Christopher Award winner *About Sarah.*

In addition to the nonfiction books she has authored, Rohrer's previous fictional titles, *Merry's Christmas; Virtually Mine; Bright Christmas; What Laurel Sees; Bridle My Heart: Second Chance Cowboys;* and *Gifted: a love story* are part of her series of *Redeeming Romance* novels, an anthology of inspirational love stories in various genres, adapted from Rohrer's original screenplays.

The Beautiful World is Rohrer's contemporary take on Porter's underlying classic, *Just David*, and Rohrer's adapted motion picture script. It is Rohrer's ardent hope to bring *The Beautiful World* to life on the screen.

About the Author of

Just David

Eleanor H. Porter

Born Eleanor Emily Hodgman in 1868, this highly esteemed twentieth-century American author hailed from New Hampshire. An avid and well-trained musician, she became known as an accomplished concert and choir singer.

Following her marriage to businessman John L. Porter, the couple settled in Massachusetts where she embarked on what would become a passionate and prolific life's work as a writer.

Just David received an auspicious welcome upon its publication, ranking second in bestselling novels throughout the United States of America in July of 1916. Porter's beloved inspirational novel has since been transcribed into Braille and translated into Chinese and Russian.

Before and after *Just David*, Porter authored many other books, including her previous and most familiar novel, *Pollyanna* (ranking eighth among U.S. bestsellers in 1913 and second in 1914). *Pollyanna* enjoyed 47 printings and became a classic family film. Porter continued to write until just weeks prior to her passing due to a severe chill in 1920.

Eleanor H. Porter was widely beloved, not only for the way her books endeared her to children and adults of all ages across the globe, but also for her winsome, joyful spirit. The faith, hope, and love abounding in her own life resonated through her infectious characters.

The Lord's Prayer, *Eternal Goodness*, *In the Wonderful Land of Peace*, and *Abide with Me* were sung as Porter was lovingly laid to rest, bound for "the far country" *Just David* echoes from *the Bible*, that heavenly home Porter wrote of, ruled over by a Great King.

CHRISTMAS REDEEMING ROMANCES BY SUSAN ROHRER

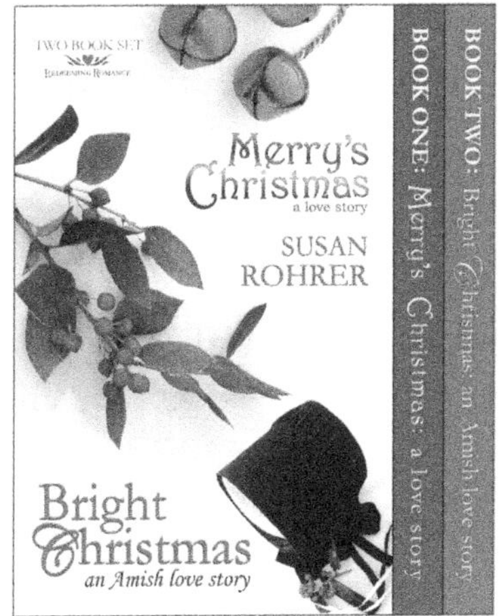

Other Redeeming Romances by Susan Rohrer

NONFICTION BOOKS BY SUSAN ROHRER

A Final Note Before We Say Goodbye

Dear Reader,

Thanks so much for the time we've spent together as you've read this book. I hope you enjoyed reading it as much as I did writing it.

Would you be so kind to post a quick review? Just go to this book's page on Amazon. You'll get to share your reading experience with family, friends, as well as other readers across the world, and I'll truly appreciate your feedback.

Gratefully,
Susan Rohrer